FRAGRANT JADE

FRAGRANT JADE

by

ALICE MARGARET HUGGINS

Illustrated by

MARYBELLE KIMBALL

BROADMAN PRESS

NASHVILLE, TENNESSEE

Printed in the United States of America

TO

DR. O. HOUGHTON LOVE

THE DR. LO

WHO WASN'T THANKED WHEN HE SHOULD HAVE BEEN

CHAPTER ONE

"LITTLE CROOKED-FOOT," everybody always called her. From the time she was born, one foot had always been bent over. When she played with other children, they laughed at the way she ran on the side of her foot. So she grew accustomed to playing by herself. Often she sat in the dust outside the courtyard gate and tossed little stones while she sang an old tune her grandfather had taught her. Or she brought a broken gourd full of water and mixing it with the dust by the road, made mud cakes, and mud sheep, and fat mud men.

Her home was on the main road through the village. Travelers often passed. Sometimes they were riding on donkeys. Sometimes they were riding on heavy two-wheeled carts loaded with grain to sell in the small city eight miles away. In the fall, farmers pushed great wheelbarrows loaded with Chinese cabbage or sweet potatoes, going to the same market. There was often something to look at. And if it should be a wedding procession or a funeral, Little Crooked-foot would run in to call her mother to come and enjoy the sight.

Mrs. Chou was a small, lively woman with bright eyes and neat shining black hair. She wore a short, dark blue cotton jacket and black cotton trousers, made baggy by being tied at the ankles by a smooth black band. She was always busy, cooking, washing, or sewing for the men folk. Little Crooked-foot knew how to help with almost all the tasks in the house. She could feed the five or six hens her mother kept, and shoo them into their coop at night. She could sweep the yard as well as anyone, or the room either. She could gather twigs from under the big trees along the road and push them slowly into the fire under the porridge kettle. She could wash the bowls and chopsticks. She could sew on a patch that her mother had basted.

Their house, like everybody else's, was built of sun-dried brick and was a straight little one-story building that filled most of the

1

north side of a square yard with a high mud wall around it. It was easy to see that the house was four rooms long. There was only one door. It opened into the second room from the east end. That was the kitchen.

But whenever the weather was warm enough, a great deal of the housework was done in the yard. They even cooked their food under a little shed between the house and the east courtyard wall, at a sort of outdoor fireplace. Fuel was kept in the yard, and the farm implements, too. That was where the dog, Spot, had his small house. The yard was back porch and woodshed and barn, all in one, and most of the time it was not very neat, in spite of the fact that it was swept every morning with a bundle of twigs for a broom.

In the village of West Market there had never been a chance for girls to learn to read and write. A little group of boys chanted their old-fashioned lessons to an old-fashioned teacher every day in the village temple from daylight to dark. Most of the children never thought of going to school. But the fall after Little Crooked-foot was ten, a primary school for girls was opened at the "Jesus Church," only a few doors away from her home. Nobody in her family had ever been inside the church. Her father, of course, knew the neighbors who went there, but he never went himself or let his sons go, and he never gave anyone a chance to tell him anything about what people did there.

Besides, he disapproved of girls learning to read, and so he talked against the new school. He was a big hard-working farmer who seldom smiled and never joked. But he took such good care of his little patch of land that his family always had enough to eat, except in years when The Heavenly Grandfather sent no rain at all.

Little Crooked-foot never knew how her mother managed to secure from her father both permission to attend and coppers for tuition, but on the very day when all the village girls from the six-year-olds to those in their teens began the first lesson in the first reader, she, too, was taken by her mother and turned over to the teacher.

The schoolroom was as big as two of the rooms at home. The walls had been freshly whitewashed, and thin white paper freshly pasted over the windows. The brick floor had been swept very clean. Desks for two and benches for two stood in straight rows, still empty.

It seemed as though all the women of the village were in the church-yard, all of them wearing their best clothes and shouting polite remarks to all of the others All the girls were there, too, bashfully standing with their mothers and not saying very much because they were wondering what it would be like to go to school.

At the front of the schoolroom, just inside the door, sat the new teacher, Miss Wang. She was young and short and rather roly-poly, dressed in a very clean, light blue cotton jacket and a black silk skirt. She had a friendly smile for each one who went in. She asked each girl's name and age, and took the tuition money.

"What is your honorable daughter's name?" she asked Little Crooked-foot's mother when it was their turn.

"Will the honorable teacher please give her a student name? She has only a baby name," Mrs. Chou answered. Little Crooked-foot was glad her mother did not tell the new teacher what it was.

"Has she an older sister so that this name must be like hers?" The teacher asked this because Chinese sisters have one name in common. It is as though the girls in an American family were named Mary Ann, Mary Jane, Mary Lou, Mary Pat, and so on.

"No," said Mrs. Chou, "she is our only little girl."

"And therefore very precious," said Miss Wang. "Suppose we call her Jade—Fragrant Jade. How do you like that?"

It was a beautiful name!

After that, every day, dressed in clean, bright blue cotton jacket and black cotton trousers, she went to study. She was tiny for her age, hardly taller than girls two or three years younger than she. Bangs lay smoothly across her forehead above bright, quick, black eyes. Her straight black hair hung neatly in one big braid down her back. Busily she practiced writing Chinese characters on her slate and then wrote them carefully on paper with a brush pen. She studied arithmetic, and a book called *General Information*. She never found the lessons hard.

Of all the things she learned, the one she liked best was music, and often in the evenings she would sing for her mother and her grandfather. Her two big brothers, who had never in their lives spent a day in school, grinned with pride as they listened. Her father scolded. He said they all spoiled her, paying attention to such nonsense. Even if she was a runt, a girl of ten or eleven ought to be doing needlework. He said she had no need to learn anything except what her mother could teach her.

Miss Wang had the girls sing every day at school, and on Sunday they sang even more. All the songs were new to Fragrant Jade, but it never took her more than a week to learn the words, no matter how many there were, and she sang them all at home. Her grandfather

liked best "Jesus Loves Me." Second Brother would never let her
stop until she had sung "Bringing in the Sheaves." Mrs. Chou said
the ones with the most stanzas were the best, and she would ask for
the longest one Fragrant Jade knew, "How Firm a Foundation."
Mr. Chou never asked for any of them. But he continued to let her
go to school. Fragrant Jade loved everything about her life as a
student.

There was one difficulty. Only three grades were offered in the
little school. In the summer after they had finished three years, Fragrant Jade's classmates prepared to leave their village and go to the
near-by city to enter the boarding school Miss Wang told them about.
True Pearl, who was always Fragrant Jade's seatmate, and the Chen
sisters, Glorious Virtue and Clear Virtue, talked about nothing else.

When Fragrant Jade's father heard of their plans, he declared he
would never waste a cent to pay his daughter's way to such a place.
At first she hoped that by some miracle he would change his mind.
Gradually she had to give up the idea of going with her friends. Finally the day came when the other girls went away without her. They
could keep on studying, she thought sadly, but for her, Fragrant Jade,
there were to be no more happy days in a schoolroom. It seemed all
too clear to her that at thirteen she had nothing left to live for. She
wandered from the house to the yard and back again into the house.
Her mother did not say anything about it, but she made the things
Fragrant Jade liked best to eat. Their appetizing fragrance filled the
rooms. Fragrant Jade knew her mother meant to comfort her, but
she could not swallow the good food.

Her father was the head of his household in the old-fashioned way.
She would not have dared to tease him for anything, least of all for
something about which he had often expressed disapproval. So far
as she could see, her education was over, and there was nothing she
could do about it. She was not remembering gratefully that in the
past three years she had enjoyed something that very few Chinese
girls experienced. She thought only of the next step, the boarding
school, and how badly she wanted to study there. Her disappoint-
ment was so great that it was like a sickness. She could not help
showing it, and she was afraid her father would scold her. He paid
no attention.

Two or three such weary days passed, days that seemed to her
endless, because they led to a future of that same dreary emptiness.
Then after supper Fragrant Jade heard her mother say to her husband, "We have only one girl-child, and she alone of our family can

read and write. Why can't you send her where she'll get learning, since she longs for it so?"

"Talking about that again!" Mr. Chou shouted.

"Everyone says she does her lessons better than most."

"Foolishness!"

"I know it takes money, but even at home we have to feed her, and the crops are good this year."

"She's a cripple," he stormed, "and too small to do hard work. To make up for that she ought to cook and sew better than other girls. Instead of giving her proper training, you let her waste her time on books! The first thing you know, nobody will be able to find a mother-in-law willing to have such a worthless, handless creature in her house."

"She can cook and sew as well as any thirteen-year-old in the village. And she does well with book learning, too, even if she is a cripple."

"That foot!" he snorted, eagerly taking up the subject his wife had offered. "I know what'll happen! Someone there at the school will make a fuss about it. I've seen that place. There's a foreign-devil doctor in the same yard with the school. Don't you know what people say he does? He'll claim he can 'fix' her foot by cutting it. Of course it can't be 'fixed' when she was born that way. She's not to go near the place."

Fragrant Jade shivered. She didn't want her foot cut. As long as she could remember she had heard the neighbor women tell stories about the foreign doctor. But how she wanted to go to school! Surely, if she went there, by keeping a sharp lookout she could avoid the dangerous man.

Her mother had the same idea. "No, no," she promised hurriedly, "she won't let the foreign doctor touch her."

"Women don't know anything! You've never been there."

"She will only read her books, as she has been doing here."

"No! I tell you! It would be throwing money away." He shouted louder, but Fragrant Jade thought his voice was not so angry as before. She watched his face.

"We have to feed her, wherever she is," Mrs. Chou repeated. "It costs very little more at the school. And see how badly she wants to go! The child makes herself sick wanting it. She has eaten nothing for three days."

Much as she wanted to go, Fragrant Jade could not see that it would do any good to keep on arguing with her father. Tears rolled

down her cheeks. What was the use of saying anything more about it?

"She can't have everything she wants," Mr. Chou growled.

Mrs. Chou never seemed to be afraid of him, no matter how cross he sounded. She went right on. "I want it, too! Neither of our sons can read. One of our children ought to get learning, and she can do it, even if she is only a girl."

"What are you talking about? Everyone knows a girl couldn't be a scholar."

Fragrant Jade sat on the edge of the brick bed and with the toe of her good foot followed the lines between the bricks of the floor. A big tear splashed onto the front of her cotton coat. She knew her father was right. The Chinese people had always had scholars, even before the days of Confucius and Mencius. But the scholars were men. "I couldn't expect to become a scholar," she thought, "but, Oh! how I wish I could just go to school, to be with the other girls, and spend the day reading and writing." Her throat felt tight, and another big tear dropped onto her jacket.

Mrs. Chou had not answered her husband.

He cleared his throat. No one said anything, and after a little he cleared his throat again.

Finally he waved his hand at his wife for silence, just as though she had been talking all the time, and shouted violently, *"Te la! Te la!* All right! All right! I suppose I might as well give up one time as another. You'll nag at me until I let her."

"And the money?" Mrs. Chou asked breathlessly.

"Just this one term—through the last moon of this year. After that I won't waste another copper on your silly notion of trying to make a scholar out of a girl."

But he meant she could go!

How fast Fragrant Jade and her mother worked that evening! They got everything ready—her narrow mattress, her comforter, her school clothes. She supposed she would be too excited to sleep, but before she knew she had dropped off, it was morning, the wonderful morning when she could go away to school.

After her father gave permission for her to go, he showed his disapproval by ignoring her. Before she was up, he and Second Brother had gone to work in the fields. Fragrant Jade felt his displeasure less because her mind was awhirl with the excitement of leaving. She was getting what she wanted above everything else, the chance to go to school, and her mother was rejoicing with her. She was satisfied with that.

On the donkey's back they spread the heavy canvas bag that held Fragrant Jade's bedding and clothes. She sat perched on top. Big Brother would have to walk the eight miles to the city. She knew that her grandfather and her mother were standing in the gateway watching her until she was out of sight, but she could not turn to take a last look. She had to hold tightly not to fall off.

Fragrant Jade had never been away from West Market before. She bounced along as the donkey trotted between fields of ripening millet and corn. Her big brother ran behind, shouting orders to the donkey. Fragrant Jade wished she could be a fairy and fly to the city. The patient little donkey seemed to creep. Yet her brother had to run to keep up, and the sun was scarcely more than half way up the sky when they came into sight of the city wall.

Big Brother had often come to market with his father, and he knew where the school was, outside the south city gate. When the two arrived there, it took Big Brother only a few minutes to pay the precious dollars he had brought for her tuition and board, and to turn her over to the school. When he said to Fragrant Jade, "I'm going," and started for the door, she bowed deeply in farewell, as she ought, and he bowed in reply. Outside, without delay, he jumped on the donkey and away he went.

As she turned back from watching him start, suddenly, with no warning, Fragrant Jade wanted to cry. The place was so big! It was full of strangers! She did not dare to look at the two teachers in the office with her. She looked instead at the floor, and there was her crooked little foot! How had she ventured to come where everyone would make fun of her, an ignorant country girl, and a cripple at that? She turned again to call her brother back, but the donkey, headed homeward, had already carried him beyond the sound of her voice.

"We'll leave the baggage here," one of the teachers said. "It'll be all right. You may go right to class, since you are several days late."

Now that she was here, Fragrant Jade dreaded meeting so many strange girls, and suddenly she was even more afraid of a new teacher. She had never studied with anyone but dear Miss Wang. What if the teacher in the big school should make fun of her or dislike her or scold when she made a mistake? Reluctantly she limped along behind the woman who was leading her to an open door. She could think of nothing but her crooked foot as she entered the room and felt scores of eyes on her. She could not look at them.

"Teacher-mother Chao," the woman with her said, "this is a new girl, Fragrant Jade. She has just come in from West Market."

Fragrant Jade bowed deeply, and then, with an effort, she ventured to look at the new teacher. What a surprise! She saw a little, frail, old woman, older than her mother, and she could not remember ever having seen so sweet a smile nor such beautiful eyes. A warm feeling took the place of the frantic fluttering in her heart.

"We are glad to see you," the teacher-mother said in a soft, gentle voice. "Would you like to sit with one of your West Market friends? She will show you the lessons."

In her fright, Fragrant Jade had forgotten that True Pearl and the Chen girls would be in this very room. In less than a minute she was seated by True Pearl, just as if she were in the little school at home. From the next seat, Glorious Virtue and Clear Virtue smiled at her while the little old teacher went on explaining the lesson.

Fragrant Jade tried to listen to what the teacher-mother was saying. She looked hard at True Pearl's book. But she got nothing out of it. She was sure all those strange girls were staring at her, and it made her very uncomfortable. She had wanted to come so badly! Now that she was here, even the gentleness of the teacher, and the feeling of True Pearl's friendly fingers tightly clasping her hand could not entirely keep her from being conscious of how small and new she was.

CHAPTER TWO

HER CHEEKS BURNING WITH EMBARRASSMENT, Fragrant Jade sat humped over the book True Pearl was sharing with her. She feared to meet the curious gaze of the girls across the aisle. When she could endure her discomfort no longer, she peeked at them. They were listening to the teacher, and their eyes were intently on their books. They seemed to have forgotten her! Since they were not looking at her, she was not afraid to look at them. She stopped trying to listen, and began to take in her surroundings.

How pretty the room was! It was larger than the one she was used to at West Market, and much lighter because, instead of paper windows, here all were of glass. Above the blackboards, on all the walls, were bright framed pictures—some of baby animals with their mothers, and others of strange foreign children. On the double desks, in front of each girl was her ink slab, and by it a little bottle of water for mixing her ink. Almost every bottle held a bright flower or two. Fragrant Jade had never thought of keeping flowers in her water bottle, but she liked the gay effect in the room. On the teacher's desk was a big bunch of zinnias, and at the other end stood a row of books with a little sign that said, "Learn your lesson first."

Fragrant Jade counted her classmates: thirty-six. They had on bright-flowered cotton jackets and black cotton trousers, and their long black braids were tied with pretty bright yarn. No one wore rouge as girls do out in the little villages, but most of them had at least one earring. One was dressed in dull gray, with white cloth sewed over her shoes, and white yarn on her braid. "I wonder who died at her house so that she has to wear mourning," Fragrant Jade thought idly. Many of the pupils were fourteen or fifteen years old. Fragrant Jade could guess why. Like the students at West Market, they were not city folk, but country girls who had lived where they had grown to ten or eleven before they had ever got a chance to start to school.

In the front seat sat a very small person. Fragrant Jade took a closer look. A boy! The short-cropped hair, the long blue student's coat—somebody must have decided to send his small son to the girls' school. Just then the little fellow looked around and gave Fragrant Jade a friendly grin that showed a dimple in each cheek. He looked as though he would be fun.

As each girl recited, Fragrant Jade had a good chance to see what kind of student she was. One she instantly disliked. The girl's name was Wu. She was a tall gawky creature who did not stand up straight. She stumbled over the words of her lesson, and when she was corrected, she pouted and refused to say anything at all. Fragrant Jade liked the others. Whenever she caught their glance, their eyes were friendly.

A big bell in the courtyard boomed. "It's time for assembly," True Pearl whispered.

Holding Fragrant Jade's hand tightly, she led the way out of their schoolroom to a place where steps went up. Fragrant Jade had never seen anything like it. The building had another layer on top of these rooms. She and True Pearl waited at one side while chattering big girls from other classes went by, climbing the stairs and disappearing through a doorway. Behind them came a fat foreign woman. Fragrant Jade recognized her the minute she saw her as the one who had visited the West Market school in the spring, and had talked about this boarding school. Her name was Miss Ho. Fragrant Jade almost smiled to herself to think how frightened she had been when she saw the person for the first time. Now the foreign teacher was only one more among many strange things.

Miss Ho's hair was not black like Chinese hair, but a faded reddish brown, and instead of lying straight and smooth, it curled so that it looked as though it had not been combed. Her eyes were blue, and that made her face look pale, except that it was reddish, too. In addition, she had on a bright cotton dress with a pattern of red and blue—much too bright for a grown-up lady, and made as differently as could be from any Chinese garment. Altogether she was very odd, but she seemed not to know it.

She stopped. "You're a new girl, aren't you?" she asked in a friendly way. "What's your name?"

"My name is Chou, and I just came from West Market this morning."

"Oh, yes, I remember you, Fragrant Jade. I'm glad you've come after all. You're not too late." She smiled, and then frowned. "Don't stand on the side of your foot like that, even if you are embarrassed. You'll make it grow crooked."

Fragrant Jade could not speak. She could not even swallow. How could she confess to the foreign teacher, in front of all those listening girls, that she stood on the side of her foot because she was a cripple?

True Pearl spoke for her. "She has to stand that way. Her foot has always been like that."

"Oh! I'm sorry!" The foreign teacher sounded sorry, but she was plainly interested, too. "We'll ask the doctor if he can't operate on it, and make it straight for you."

A chill struck Fragrant Jade in the middle of her stomach. She let True Pearl lead her up the steps and into the big assembly room. She no longer cared that for the first time in her life she was in the top layer of a house. She paid no attention to all the big and little girls. Stiff and numb she sat on her bench, hearing hardly a word that was said, she was so frightened. Her father had predicted that when the foreign-devil doctor saw her foot he would want to "fix" it. And now, almost as soon as she had stepped into the school, the foreign teacher planned to hunt trouble for her: "We'll ask the doctor if he can't operate on it."

The neighbors in West Market loved to tell about the foreign doctors. They put a person to sleep, and cut his body open, and took out anything they chose. They had in their hospitals saws and scissors and knives of all kinds with which to cut people. A man in West Market had a friend who knew someone who had seen them! And people said that sometimes those doctors took out people's eyes and used them for medicine!

Fragrant Jade felt very small. What could she do?

By the end of chapel she had figured out that the first thing was to keep the foreign teacher from saying anything at all to the doctor about the foot. She would tell the foreign teacher right out that she did not want a straight foot. After that, she must take pains not to be seen by the foreign doctor. If he did not know she was there, he could not harm her. The most important thing of all was that he must never get a chance to put her to sleep. So long as she was awake, she could watch that he did not cut her foot. He might just cut it off! It was much better to have a crooked foot, unpleasant as that was, than it would be to have no foot at all. She would talk to the foreign teacher, and she would stay out of sight of the doctor. When she had made this plan, she felt a little better.

Chapel was followed by recess. Everybody came down the stairs again. Fragrant Jade had never tried to come down so many steps. With one hand she hung onto True Pearl and with the other she steadied herself by feeling her way along the wall by the stairs. It was much harder to come down than it had been to go up, and she was not the only one of the small girls who came down *"bung, bung, bung,"* making a lot of noise as their feet hit the steps.

Clear Virtue and Glorious Virtue, True Pearl and Fragrant Jade walked together, arms around each other, while they looked over the school. The courtyards were full of zinnias, asters, and four o'clocks, and they were shaded in many places by big willows and locust trees. Here and there were the two-layered classroom buildings that Fragrant Jade thought she must remember to tell her mother and grandfather about. The dormitories looked natural. They were like the homes in West Market, built three or more little rooms in a row, on each side of a square yard. The paper windows in these were fresh and clean. Fragrant Jade was proud that she belonged to such a fine-looking school.

"Dozens of girls are new like us," True Pearl said. "Lots of them came without knowing a soul in this place! It's much nicer that there are four of us from the same village."

Fragrant Jade was thinking the same thing. Now that she was with her West Market friends, she was not so frightened of so many strangers. "Who is the little boy up in front?" she remembered to ask.

The other three girls laughed and laughed. "She fooled us too! She isn't a boy! She's the only child, and her mother says she must learn to honor her parents the way a son would. So she fixes her up like a boy. Her name is 'Eminent Wisdom.' Nobody but the teacher-mother calls her that. She's too mischievous. We all call her just 'Boy.' "

"There's one girl I don't like, the one named Wu."

"She's spoiled," one of the Chen girls started, and her sister went right on with the sentence, "because her father's rich, and she has too much money to spend. He sits in the front seat in church. You'll see him. He's all right. He's not silly like her."

"But you're right," True Pearl said, "the other girls are nice. And nobody ever saw a nicer teacher. Oh, how glad I am you've come."

At noon, a man who worked for the school carried Fragrant Jade's bedding roll for her to the Third Court where she was to live. It was not far from the main buildings of the school. He banged on the gate, and when the two of them stepped inside, they found an ordinary

Chinese residence: on the north side of the courtyard five paper-windowed rooms in a row faced south, and on the west side four smaller ones faced east. The yard itself was bright with red and yellow flowers, and under some old trees, stools and benches were ready for anyone who wanted to study or sew out-of-doors.

A dozen people came rushing out of several doorways. "You're to be in my room," the biggest girl called cordially, coming on the run to carry the bedding roll.

One, a young lady, wore the light blue jacket and full black skirt of a teacher. Fragrant Jade walked toward her and bowed.

"I'm Miss Chang," the teacher said. She nodded her head toward the big girl carrying the bedding roll. "Bright Wisdom will be your Big Sister, and tell you the rules."

Fragrant Jade soon learned that one of the five rooms in the larger building belonged to the teacher, and that the other four were full of girls, four in each, so that there were sixteen students in the Third Court "family." Dining room, kitchen, and bathroom were on the west side of the court, where the fourth room belonged to Li Nai-nai, the woman who managed the kitchen, prepared their noon meal, and watched the house while they were in class.

"We cook our own breakfasts and suppers," Bright Wisdom told Fragrant Jade. "You'll be assigned to one of the groups. But don't worry. You'll have an older girl to help you. In the Third Court you'll never have harder tasks than you can do, Little Sister." Bright Wisdom, who was in the top class in the school, had charge of everything about their room. She was big and strong, and taller than the teacher. She was not particularly pretty, but she had made Fragrant Jade love her already.

Fragrant Jade's other two roommates were new students like herself. Dream Cloud was fourteen and in the sixth-year class. Like-an-Orchid was a very tiny girl, just starting in the first grade.

Half the room next the windows, was taken by the brick bed, a platform about as high as a chair, that ran the whole way across the room. It was covered by a yellow straw matting, and brightened by a pile of folded comforters at each end, against the walls. Standing in the middle of the wall opposite it, was the only real piece of furniture in the room, a table with four drawers in it. Fragrant Jade was assigned one of them to hold her small articles, like comb and pencils. Behind the door were four shelves, covered by a curtain. All three roommates helped take from the bedding roll Fragrant Jade's comforters to heap with theirs on the brick bed, and her clothes, which they piled, neatly folded, on the one empty shelf. Her things were unpacked and put away in less than ten minutes.

Lunch was cabbage soup, with big hunks of corn bread to eat with it. It was so tasty and Fragrant Jade was so hungry after her long ride, that she drank three bowls!

The afternoon in the fourth grade classroom passed pleasantly. The girls practiced Chinese writing, and after that Teacher-mother Chao told them about an unbelievably strange kind of people who live near the North Pole.

After school came games. Fragrant Jade was standing at one side watching the other students dash about in "Kitty and Mousie" when suddenly she remembered what the foreign teacher had said about her foot. She wondered whether, if she did not play with the rest, that fact might be made an excuse for operating on her foot. Reluctantly she joined the circle, and right away found she had become the Kitty. The Wu girl was Mousie. Fragrant Jade chased her back and forth and round and round. The girl was big, and seemed awkward, but she was quick. Fragrant Jade could not come anywhere near her. Her face grew hot on account of embarrassment, as well as on account of so much exertion on such a warm day, but she kept on running and running, doing her very best, yet always far behind.

The Wu girl, lacking competition, began to tease by running first one foolish way and then another, and finally by mimicking Fragrant Jade limping about on one side of her foot. It was not the first time a playmate had done exactly that very thing to tease her. Fragrant Jade merely blinked back the tears and kept on running.

A few girls giggled and then someone shouted "Shame!" and two or three big ones caught the Wu girl and stopped her. The game was broken up, and before another could be started, the bell rang. Fragrant Jade was glad to get away to the quiet of the Third Court.

In the fun of cooking supper, she forgot about her foot. The squad on duty made millet porridge. That was easy. Fragrant Jade had learned from her mother how to prepare many dishes more difficult than that. The huge iron kettle full of bubbling golden gruel filled the room with an appetizing smell, just like supper at home. Supper at home! What would her mother be doing now? What time of day had it been when Big Brother got back, and what had he reported about her school? Was her father still cross about spending money in what he considered a foolish way?

These questions stayed in Fragrant Jade's mind as the sixteen members of the Third Court settled down for evening study hall. Between her eyes and her new books pictures kept rising—of her mother bustling around the house, of her grandfather sitting in the sunshine, and of Miss Wang and the little West Market School. She tried to prepare her lessons, but she could not see the words through the tears. She swallowed and then swallowed again. She was not going to cry! She wanted to be here! Her father had said she should stay at home. No! Of all the places in the world this was the one where she was determined to be. Yet the tears kept coming. She brushed them away roughly with the back of her hand.

Suddenly somebody began to howl. "Ma! Ma! I want my mother! I'm afraid of the nighttime!" It was six-year-old Like-an-Orchid.

Everybody stopped studying, and all began to talk at once. "Don't cry!" "I'll get you a piece of candy." "Keep still!" "You can't go to your mother now, it's too far." "Nobody else cries. Be a big girl."

After a few minutes of such confusion, Miss Chang's voice scolded, "Do keep still! It's time for evening prayers, and nobody can hear anything."

Like-an-Orchid would not listen to any of them. The more they urged her to stop crying the more she wanted her mother.

Bright Wisdom picked up her little roommate and began to sing, "Jesus Loves Me." At once other girls joined in the song. Before they had finished the first stanza, Like-an-Orchid's crying was drowned out. The girls sang another song and then another. Tired little Like-an-Orchid fell asleep in Bright Wisdom's arms. Fragrant Jade felt better, too, comforted by the same hymns that Miss Wang had taught her. After a while Miss Wang led them quietly in an evening prayer.

Fragrant Jade's first day at boarding school was over.

CHAPTER THREE

THE SEPTEMBER DAYS were sunny and warm. The schoolgirls studied inside the courtyards or out on the grounds. Between the school and the city wall flowed the shallow moat which the girls called "the river." Tall, graceful old willow trees shaded its grassy banks. It was the most beautiful and peaceful spot Fragrant Jade had ever seen. Every day she and True Pearl sat on the grass between the dike and the moat, and studied their lessons aloud until recalled by the ancient temple bell in the school yard. Usually the Chen girls joined them there.

On Sunday afternoon they took their hymnbooks, and leaning against a favorite tree, began to turn the pages and to sing all the songs of which they knew the tunes. After a little two or three other girls, attracted by the sound, came and sat down near by, and then later a few more came. The West Market girls paid no attention. They had been there first, but they had no objection if their schoolmates wanted to sit by the moat, too. They kept going through the books, singing every song they knew. Wherever there were words they could not read, they just sang *"hung-hung."*

Bright Wisdom was in a circle of older girls who were reading not far away. One of those in the group called, "Do you know number 216?"

Fragrant Jade and True Pearl found the song, and answered, "We know that a little." It was "In Heavenly Love Abiding."

"It's the song we like best here at our school," Bright Wisdom told them. "You start it, and we'll sing alto with you."

Fragrant Jade had never heard anybody sing alto before. She loved the sound of two tunes that went together so. She would have liked to look for another song they could sing the same way, but one of the older girls spoke as soon as they finished.

"That little girl has a lovely voice! Where did she learn to sing like that?" The girl was talking about her!

"That's Fragrant Jade, my little roommate," Bright Wisdom

19

answered. "Her first grade teacher taught her, but she must have had a voice to begin with. Fragrant Jade, sing something alone, something you know, such as—well, 'Precious Jewels' will be a good one."

The girls in the Third Court often sang it at evening prayers, so Fragrant Jade knew the song well. The dike behind them and the old city wall across the moat were like the opposite ends of a great room. She could feel that her voice was not lost. It was fun to sing there under the trees.

Everything was fun. Fragrant Jade just wished it could last forever. But often, mixed with her intense enjoyment of the autumn beauty came the anxious thought that in some way she must persuade her father to let her come back next term. He had paid her board only till Chinese New Year, and he had said he would give no more. Now that she had had a taste of boarding school, it would be harder than ever to give it up. How could she get him to change his mind?

The other worrisome thought was about her foot. She wished she could be like other girls. Some of them were so pretty! There was a big mirror in the hall, and when nobody was looking, Fragrant Jade went and stood before it. At home the only looking glass they had did not even show all of her face at once. Here she could see from head to foot. The hair was all right. The face was no worse than anybody else's face. The blue jacket and black trousers were neat and clean. But that foot! She tried to make it stand straight, but she could not fool herself. It was a crooked thing, and every time she looked at it, she thought it was uglier.

Like-an-Orchid liked stories better than anything else, and fortunately Bright Wisdom liked to tell stories. So every night, between study hall and bedtime, the three roommates listened to the tales their Big Sister told.

Like-an-Orchid's favorite was a very long one about a little boy named Joseph whose father gave him a pretty coat, and then he had a lot of trouble, but when he grew up he became a great man in a foreign country and saved all his family during a famine. Bright Wisdom told another about Mencius's mother who moved her home three times so that her son would like to go to school, and how he grew up to be a great leader in his country. She told of brave little Sun Yat Sen, and of another little boy named Samuel, and of little Washington who would not tell a lie about a cherry tree, and of young Lincoln who studied by firelight. All the heroes of her stories did something wonderful for their country. When Like-an-Orchid asked for a story about a girl, Bright Wisdom told about Joan of

Arc, or Mu Lan, or Esther. Each of them, also, had done something great for her country.

Little Like-an-Orchid said that when she grew up she was going to save her country, too. Fragrant Jade wished that she could, but she kept still. She was afraid she would never do anything so great. Bright Wisdom had never told a story about anybody important who was a cripple.

Dream Cloud asked, "Where do you get so many good stories?"

"Mostly out of books," Bright Wisdom said. "I get some of them from our school books, and some from the Bible."

"The Bible!" Dream Cloud exclaimed, as though displeased. "My father says I must never listen to it. It's nothing but superstition."

"I want the Bible stories! I want all the stories!" Like-an-Orchid cried. "Dont stop telling Bible stories because her father doesn't like them."

"All right, Little Sister. Don't make such a fuss! I'll tell you all the stories you want. But Dream Cloud, let me hear you name the superstitious stories from the Bible that you have heard me tell."

Dream Cloud thought hard. "I can't remember any story you've told that had superstition in it. They've all been like history, about boys and girls who did something good for their country when they got big."

"Perhaps your father hasn't read the Bible. It has a great deal of history in it. Read it sometime and see for yourself. Anyway, don't worry. None of the stories I'll tell will hurt you."

Fragrant Jade thought she knew which were the Bible stories, but she did not say anything. Miss Wang had often told the little West Market students about Joseph, Moses, and Samuel. Fragrant Jade was pretty sure they were in the Bible, because sometimes at Sunday school or church they were mentioned. In the West Market School she had heard about Washington and Lincoln, too, but she thought they had lived in Teacher Ho's country. She did not know about the others. The Bible was about foreigners, and most of the people in the stories were foreigners, but perhaps they were from different foreign countries. Fragrant Jade was not very sure.

One October evening Bright Wisdom announced, "Like-an-Orchid's mother has sent money for a scarf, and wants someone to knit it for her."

"Oh, let me!" Fragrant Jade cried. "Only—"

"Only what, Little Sister?"

"I'll have to learn first." She did so want to know how to knit! She had never seen it done until she came here, where everybody else was making herself something. Other girls' flashing needles fascinated her.

"Oh, that's easy," Bright Wisdom assured her comfortably. "I've seen your sewing, and your fingers aren't stupid at all. You'll be able to do this in no time."

Before the week had passed, by practicing faithfully, Fragrant Jade had learned to knit smoothly enough so that she was given the pretty new scarlet yarn. After school, Like-an-Orchid sat beside her and chattered while she watched the work on her scarf.

"There's a girl in our class who never eats any lunch. They say there isn't any food at home for her to bring. She says she's not hungry. And do you know what else she tells us? She tells us her uncle has golden chopsticks and golden ricebowls." Like-an-Orchid made a scornful face.

"Maybe he has, but doesn't give her anything."

"I don't believe it! I called her 'Golden Chopsticks,' and now all the girls call her 'Golden Chopsticks.' It makes her so mad! And she can't find any name that makes me that mad. Isn't that fun?"

Fragrant Jade saw in memory a child at West Market whom everybody had always laughed at when she tried to run, and whose only name had been "Little Crooked-foot." A fellow feeling made her pity "Golden Chopsticks." She knew what Miss Wang would say about the way Like-an-Orchid was teasing her!

"I'll tell you a story, Like-an-Orchid, and sing a song that our teacher at home taught us."

"Oh, goody! You sing better than anyone. Please do!"

"Once upon a time—" Fragrant Jade began, as though it was just a story. She told about her first day at the West Market School, how the other girls had mimicked her, and how Miss Wang stopped them and taught them their first lesson in the little new school: that it is cruel to make fun of other people's infirmities. Then she sang for Like-an-Orchid the little song Miss Wang had taught them that morning, and had them sing many times in the three years since, "Be ye kind one to another." She did not mention how much the Wu girl's teasing had hurt a few weeks before.

"Did they really make fun of your foot? The mean old things!" Like-an-Orchid scolded loyally. "You couldn't help being born that way." She had already forgotten Golden Chopsticks.

"People can't help being poor, either. Your Golden Chopsticks probably hates it as much as I hate having a crooked foot."

While talking to Like-an-Orchid, Fragrant Jade had felt with a new bitterness how very much she did hate having a club foot. As far back as she could remember she had heard the neighbor women say, "Heaven made her so. It is her fate." There was no help for it. She knew that.

She had never got around to talking to the foreign teacher, as she had planned to do on her first day at school. Apparently it was not going to be necessary. Miss Ho seemed to have forgotten her idea of asking the doctor if he could make her foot straight. Fragrant Jade was sure he could not. She was too much afraid of him to consider letting him try. She had no intention of changing her mind about that!

Besides, she felt sure her father would never give his consent. Hadn't his objection to the "foreign devil-doctor" been one of the reasons why he had not wanted her to come to the boarding school? She did not intend to do anything that could possibly displease her father. She wanted to come back to school.

Yet how many times since she had been in this new place had she felt her cheeks flush hot because strange girls stopped and stared at her limping by! It was not pleasant to think that all her life she would be looked at with such unsympathetically curious eyes. She would like a straight foot, but it was a thing she could not have.

Right beside Fragrant Jade's school was another of which Miss Wang had told the West Market children long ago. The pupils in it were foreigners—Americans, like Teacher Ho and the foreign doctor, and some from other countries Fragrant Jade did not know the names of. Sometimes she saw a few of them as she went by on the way to church. They played out on their grounds with bare arms and legs. She was thankful she did not have to do it. It was all right for boys, but her mother would not have let her go out of doors with so few clothes on. And her father! He would have been horrified at the thought. But Fragrant Jade found them interesting. She wondered if all the tales she heard about the foreign children could be true.

The boys and girls went to the same classes, played together, ate in the same dining room, even at the same table. Fragrant Jade felt a little sorry for the girls. If she had to eat at the same table with boys, she would not be able to swallow a bite. She had herself seen them walking around their grounds, a boy and a girl together. She wondered what they talked about. She was glad she did not have to walk with a boy!

One day there was a rumor that the American boys and girls would give a play in the big hall at the boys' school. Then Miss Ho came and announced it, adding, "You may all go if you like, but it will be in English, so you won't understand it. Even so, you may think it worth while to go just to see how American students put on a play."

Of course they would! Long before the play was due to begin, the girls' school filled the benches that had been assigned to them. Fragrant Jade got a seat as near as she could to Teacher Ho, hoping she might hear some comments.

"The story is called 'Seventeen,' and it's about a boy seventeen years old," Miss Ho explained.

Soon the curtain went up. On the stage were many more things than are customary for a Chinese play. It looked almost like a room in Teacher Ho's house. Fragrant Jade wished she knew what the actors were saying, but it was interesting just to watch the Americans. She looked carefully at their clothes, and at everything they did, but she could not figure out what the boy and his friends were doing.

After a while the curtain went down, and when it went up again, the stage was entirely different. Fragrant Jade asked the girl next to her, but they could not imagine what the scenery was meant to be. Teacher Ho whispered that it was the outside of an American home with a porch, and that the house was not built of bricks or plastered with mud as in North China, but made of wood cut into strips and nailed together. Fragrant Jade could hardly believe it. Wood was so expensive! How could people afford to buy enough wood to build a house? But she tried to look as though she had seen many wooden houses. She did not want Teacher Ho to lose face because her pupils did not believe she was telling the truth.

Then she was glad to hear the girl next to Miss Ho say, "I hope you won't laugh at me for being so ignorant, but I never knew before that anyone ever built a house of wood."

"Oh," Miss Ho answered calmly, "many things are different in other places. People build houses with whatever material is most convenient in their country."

All the way home, and while they were getting ready for bed, the girls talked about the play. There were widely different versions of the story.

"I'm glad I am a Chinese," was Fragrant Jade's comment, "and that we have good manners and customs handed down from ancient times."

"It's all right to be glad you are a Chinese," Bright Wisdom answered, "but you mustn't think we are the only people who have good manners and good customs. Americans have customs, too, not like ours, but not necessarily bad."

"But surely there were girls and boys all on the stage at once," Fragrant Jade objected. "Not even ignorant country people in China do that. We think it doesn't look nice."

"I know, but I've heard Miss Ho say that American boys and girls have rules, and know how they must behave," Bright Wisdom insisted. "You mustn't make up your mind that they are uncultured until you know more about them. When you've studied some English, you'll find they have a kind of politeness. They say thank you more than we do."

Fragrant Jade was not entirely convinced, but she thought she must try to be fair. "I like Teacher Ho all right," she said, "but what about doctors who came all the way to China to cut up people who didn't want them to?"

On the next afternoon Teacher-mother Chao showed the class some pictures of diseased eyes, and explained what trachoma is, and how it is spread by careless use of other people's towels and washbasins, and by rubbing one's eyes with dirty fingers. The more she talked, the more Fragrant Jade's eyes itched and hurt. She was sure she had the horrid disease.

While they were still looking at the pictures, into the room stepped two people dressed in white. One was the foreign doctor! Fragrant Jade looked toward the open door. If she tried to get away. . . . No, she would fail. If she started across the room, the doctor would see her limp, and want to operate on her foot. Small and fearful, she sat pressed against True Pearl's solid little arm.

The doctor and the Chinese nurse with him had been examining the eyes of the big girls in the other rooms, and now in turn they came to the fourth grade. The doctor sat in a good light near the door, and the girls went to him by groups so that when he turned each girl's eyelids back, several others could see. They guessed, "She has it," or "She hasn't it," and waited for Dr. Lo to say whether they were right. Some of the new students, like Fragrant Jade, were afraid of the doctor, but the old students seemed to like him, and acted as if this were just a new game. They soon learned to recognize both bad cases and eyes that were entirely well. The doctor kept stopping to wash his hands, though anyone could see that they were perfectly clean.

Hidden behind the others, Fragrant Jade felt sure he had not noticed her. When her turn came, she carefully squeezed into place

without letting him see her limp, and stood there stiff and still. The doctor smelled faintly of medicine. His fingers were gentle but firm, and although it did not feel good to have her eyelids turned back, she could not say that he really hurt her. It was a relief to hear the girls shout, "She hasn't it!" The doctor's brown eyes laughed into hers, and he said, "You're glad!" as if he were, too. He did not look as bad as people said he was. Just the same, Fragrant Jade moved away from him as fast as she could, and went back to her seat. She was lucky this time.

When the examinations were over, the nurse read the names of all those who had the trouble, and told them to take benches to the courtyard and sit in a big circle under the old locust tree to get their first treatment. The rest of the class trooped out, too, to stand around and watch. Only Fragrant Jade and the Wu girl stayed with the teacher in the room. In a few minutes the teacher called the Wu girl's name.

"I'm not going," she said pouting and slumping down over her desk. Fragrant Jade was horrified to hear anybody speak so to a teacher.

"Oh, yes, you are," the teacher-mother answered quietly. "If trachoma is treated it doesn't spread so easily to other people, so while you are getting better yourself, you are helping to protect your classmates. Everyone who has it here must be treated."

"Doesn't the treatment hurt?"

"Of course."

"Then I don't care who catches it, I'm not going to let the doctor hurt me. I'll take my books and quit school! I'll tell my father."

Fragrant Jade gasped. The girl had already been rude beyond belief. This was even worse. She meant to threaten that her father would come and make trouble at school. Fragrant Jade looked closely at the teacher-mother to see whether she was nervous.

She was answering calmly, "You may go if you choose, of course, and certainly you would have to tell your father, because you couldn't come back until you were willing to let the doctor do for you what he thinks is best, and what is plainly for your good, even though it does hurt." She turned to the blackboard and began to write.

Fragrant Jade pretended to be reading a book, but she could see everything. The Wu girl took out all her books, and piled them carefully, first one way and then another, moving more and more slowly. Finally she began putting them away again, and when they were all in the desk, without saying anything, she sauntered out of the door and found a place on one of the benches in the yard.

Fragrant Jade sat wondering. The teacher-mother was willing to let the richest girl in their class go home and stay there if she would not take the treatment the doctor chose to give her. Suppose he should decide to try to straighten a crooked foot? What then? If Fragrant Jade should let him, her father might be so angry he would never let her come again to the school she loved more every day. If she should not, wouldn't the teacher-mother send her home for disobeying? The only safe thing was to keep the doctor from finding out that there was anything wrong with her foot.

CHAPTER FOUR

SOMETIMES TEACHER HO BROUGHT MESSAGES to the school from her country, America, which the Chinese call "The Beautiful Country." Her friends sent many bright pictures of flowers and children, and of strange things and strange places. The girls put them on the walls of their bedrooms. Sometimes there were parcels with little gifts.

One day Teacher Ho brought to the school a huge bundle of bright woolen wristlets. "It's soon going to be winter," she said, "and your American friends want you to be warm. I think there are enough for every girl who hasn't a pair already. Help me choose the right size for each of you."

The wristlets were of all colors, some of them very gay, with stripes of eight or ten brilliant colors. Fragrant Jade's turn came, and Miss Ho let her choose from all those that were left. It was hard to decide, they were all so pretty, but finally she took a pair that were purple and green and yellow. It made her feel happy just to look at them, and the wool was warm and soft.

Another day, an even more exciting gift arrived. Teacher Ho brought the big package to the assembly hall, and explained that friends in America had sent it for all the school to play with. She unwrapped an American doll as big as a baby, with eyes that went to sleep, and beautiful pink cheeks. The girls held their breath in admiration. Miss Ho showed them its odd little clothes, which she said were the kind American babies really wear. They were all white, and thin and very oddly made, altogether different from the pretty red calico ones Chinese babies wear.

The new doll lay in a basket in the corner of Teacher Ho's office, where it slept except when somebody was playing with it. The girls named it "Mei-mei," which means "Little Sister," and every day they went by twos and threes to hold her and watch her open and close her eyes. After a while they got used to the odd white clothes. Fragrant Jade often went with some classmate who was going to play with

29

Mei-mei. She had never had a doll, even when she was a little girl, and she loved this American "Little Sister."

"I wish I had some cloth," she told her roommates. "I'd make a pair of shoes for Mei-mei. She has only white knitted ones that look almost like stockings. I'd like to make her a pair of cat shoes."

"I'll give you a piece of cloth," Like-an-Orchid offered. "You know that red cloth like my trousers? I have some of that."

"That'll be exactly right," Bright Wisdom decided. "And I have a good pattern here with my other patterns. Let's start right away."

They cut out the little shoes, and Fragrant Jade sewed them with her very finest stitches. She made the cat's eyes, nose, mouth, and whiskers on the toes of the shoes, and made a tail to hang from the back. They were just like the ones Chinese babies wear.

"The old women say the cat's eyes are to see the path for the little feet, but I don't believe that, do you, Bright Wisdom, even if Mei-mei could walk, which she can't?"

"No, I'm afraid it's just a foolish saying. But surely the cat shoes are much cuter than the white ones Mei-mei is wearing."

Fragrant Jade worked so faithfully that within a week the little shoes were done. All her roommates went with her to present them to Mei-mei. Soon other girls heard about it, and had to see Mei-mei wearing her new shoes.

"Let's make her a whole outfit of Chinese clothes," someone shouted. Everybody was ready to help. The doll was so fat that the clothes were hard to fit, but the girl's fingers were nimble, and soon little Mei-mei's blue eyes, pink cheeks and white face looked out from between a red jacket and red tasseled cap.

Boy spent as much time with Mei-mei as anybody, but that was not all the playing she did. Her desk was full of ever so many things. She usually had some peanuts, or water chestnuts, or bits of hard candy, or a little parcel of watermelon seeds. She would slip a few into her pocket when she started out for recess. She knew better than to try to eat them in school. It was hard for her to find a chance to enjoy any of her playthings, because she had the front seat, and the teacher-mother could see her too well.

From where Fragrant Jade sat she could see peeking out of Boy's desk a small cloth tiger her mother had once made for her. He was of red and yellow striped cloth, about four inches long, and with such short squatty legs that his stomach nearly touched the floor. His black ears stood perky and straight, his whiskers were pink, and he had a pink tassel on the end of his tail. Most amusing of all were his round-

est-of-round eyes made of circles of yellow cloth sewed on circles of
black. Boy's eyes were round, too, so Fragrant Jade thought she and
the tiger looked as though they belonged to each other.

Teacher-mother always used Boy's right name. "Eminent Wisdom,
what are the products of our province?" she asked in geography
class.

The name sounded so great it was almost unbelievable that Boy,
short and round, should stand up, and shift from one foot to the other,
trying to answer. She rolled her big eyes at the teacher, thinking
hard. She rolled them at the class, very, very soberly. Fragrant Jade
looked at the tiger. He seemed to wink at her. Boy, for all her wise
name, did not know the products of her own province.

Boy had a black and white puppy, too, which she called "Jumpy."
Sometimes he followed her to school, and Fragrant Jade played with
him. But the teacher-mother always asked Boy to take him home
when the first bell rang.

One October morning, Dream Cloud woke up with an itching red
blotch on her face. She said she was too sick to go to school. Bright
Wisdom ran to ask the teacher what to do.

Miss Chang came and took one look. "I don't know what's the
matter," she said, "but the sooner you go to the doctor the sooner
you'll be over it."

So Dream Cloud trudged off to the hospital, and by noon, word
had come back that she must stay there so there would be no danger
that what she had might spread to her roommates.

The very next day, Fragrant Jade woke up with a headache and
and an itching red blotch on her face.

"So you're to go to the hospital, too," Bright Wisdom stated cheerfully. "Dream Cloud will be glad of your company there, but Like-an-
Orchid and I'll be lonely with two of our roommates gone."

Going to the hospital was the one thing above all others that Fragrant Jade made up her mind that she would never do. The very
thought made her head ache as badly as it had ached before. If she
went inside the place, she would be putting herself into the doctor's
power, and who knew what might happen? "No!" she told Bright
Wisdom. "No! I can't go!"

"I'm sure you'll have to, just like Dream Cloud," her big sister
answered mildly, "but I'll ask Miss Chang if you like." She ran out
and along the front of the building toward the teacher's room.

"I can't go! I won't go!" Fragrant Jade yelled after her. She
curled up on the brick bed, covered her head with the comforter, and

made herself as small as possible. Her head really did ache badly. And how hot and tired she felt!

When she heard Bright Wisdom and Miss Chang come in she paid no attention.

"Get up, Fragrant Jade, and go to the hospital right away." It was the teacher speaking.

Fragrant Jade answered from under the covers where she had hidden. "I'm practically well. I—I don't think I'll need to go." Perhaps she could talk Miss Chang out of the idea. "I had a headache, but—"

"Let me see your face."

Fragrant Jade's head came out from under the covers.

"Nearly well! You're a sight! Now run along."

She couldn't! Go to the hospital where that doctor was? She must find some way to avoid it. She thought fast. "I'll go home, and my mother'll make me well, and then I'll come right back," she suggested.

"Of course not. The hospital is the place for sick people. They get well much quicker than they do at home."

"My father won't let me." This was the first time she had been glad her father objected to the foreign doctor.

"When he brought you to school he must have promised that you'd be under the care of the doctor."

"He didn't bring me. My Big Brother brought me."

"Whoever acted for your father agreed that your health was to be in charge of Dr. Lo. Everybody's is, here at the school. Now hurry up."

"Oh!" Fragrant Jade had suddenly thought of another good excuse. "I haven't any money. I can't pay the doctor."

"The principal will help plan that." Miss Chang turned to go.

What could Fragrant Jade say? She lay back on her pillow and began to cry. She was so utterly helpless! Now that a definite order had been given, it was useless to imagine that she could avoid obeying.

Vivid in Fragrant Jade's mind was the memory of how the teacher-mother was going to let the rich Wu girl go home and stay there if she was "unwilling to let the doctor do for her what was for her own good." Oh, why did this horrid blotch have to come on her face? It would not matter to any of the other girls. No one else had a crooked foot she had to keep out of sight of the doctor. But sooner or later she would have to do what Miss Chang had told her to do.

"I don't understand you," Bright Wisdom said sympathetically, coming over and putting a hand on Fragrant Jade's shoulder. "Such a fuss about going to the hospital! As if that was anything!"

Fragrant Jade only cried harder.

"I'll tell you what," Bright Wisdom offered. "I'll go with you, and we'll find Dream Cloud. But we'll have to start pretty soon, because I'll have to get back to class. Come on!"

There was no doubt that it would be easier if Big Sister went with her. Reluctantly Fragrant Jade prepared to go. Her head ached, and her face burned and itched. Carrying a few little things in a bundle, in silence she limped along, two or three steps behind Bright Wisdom, all the way to the hospital. She did not see the glorious yellow leaves on the willows overhead, nor the scarlet and crimson vines on the gray brick walls of the buildings they passed. Her heart was heavy with fear of what the doctor would say when he saw her crooked foot.

Dream Cloud was lying in a white bed.

"I've brought you a companion," Bright Wisdom called to her.

"I'm almost well already, but I'm glad you've come," Dream Cloud said, with a smile of welcome for Fragrant Jade. "See? The bed opposite mine is empty. Let's ask Nurse Chi to give it to you."

An hour later, Fragrant Jade was lying in the cool white bed Dream Cloud had pointed out. She had had a bath and was dressed in bright-colored fresh pajamas. She had to confess to herself that she was already more comfortable.

When Dr. Lo came, he was full of jokes, and his fingers were gentle as he put medicine on her burning face and tied it up with clean white cloths. He never so much as looked in the direction of her feet. "We'll have you well in a day or two," he promised. "Take a nap whenever you feel like it, or tell each other funny stories if you know any, or sing if you want to," he said as he left.

"I'll have Fragrant Jade sing to me," Dream Cloud told him. "She can sing like a bird."

They sang and ate and laughed and slept. Fragrant Jade kept her crooked foot carefully under covers, but nobody seemed to notice it. Nurse Chi seemed always to be coming in with good things to eat or drink, and she always had something jolly to say every time she came. Being in the hospital was not a bit like Fragrant Jade had expected.

The next day, both of the girls felt perfectly well, so Nurse Chi said they might play out-of-doors. They sat in the sunny courtyard and watched patients come to the hospital. Some rode in rickshas, but many of them walked slowly in, and sat down wearily on one of the many benches where they could wait their turns with the doctor. There were men on crutches, and some with their heads tied with white bandages like Fragrant Jade's and Dream Cloud's. They must have come to the hospital before. Some covered their eyes from the bright sun. Worried-looking mothers carried sick pale babies. While the girls watched, some people came carrying a sick man on a door. They had tied ropes to it so that it swung between men walking on both sides.

"I wouldn't have supposed there were so many sick people any-where," Fragrant Jade remarked.

"Of course there are! These are only a few of the sick people in the city. Most folks don't come to the foreign doctor. They're afraid of him. My father says the American doctor is all right for diseases on the outside of the body, but not for those on the inside. Chinese people are made differently inside from Americans, my father says."

Fragrant Jade thought a moment. "Perhaps that's why Dr. Lo has had such good luck with us," she said. "Our disease is on the outside, and we're getting well fast."

"Of course that's the reason. These American doctors know very little about Chinese medicine. They never feed people tiger's heart to make them brave, and my father says they don't even know that eating a little of the mad dog's hair will cure a mad dog's bite. My father says there are ever so many things that everybody in China knows, that these foreign doctors never heard of at all, and yet they come here and try to cure us. My father says that sometimes they do jab their patients with needles, but it's not the same as when a Chinese doctor does it. They know only a few of the right places to jab, so they have to put medicine into their needles."

The two girls watched sick people come and go until Nurse Chi called them to come and eat lunch.

Every morning after breakfast the doctor went around to see all his patients. The next morning, Fragrant Jade and Dream Cloud were free to go out into the yard, but when it was nearly time for the doctor to talk to them, they sat on the stools by their beds and waited for him. Fragrant Jade kept her crooked foot carefully hidden. She was sure that the doctor had never seen it.

When he had finished looking at the red blotch on her face, he remarked in a pleased tone, "We're coming along fast." Then, as if he had known about it all the time, he added, "So you were born with a club foot. Want to let me see it?"

Fragrant Jade was so frightened that she could not speak. She had hoped she could get away from her stay in the hospital without his finding out about her foot. The next thing, he would say he wanted to operate on it!

But he surprised her. "Oh, all right," he said as though it did not matter at all. "Never mind. I just thought that being a schoolgirl you might want it straightened. You're all so interested in making yourselves pretty."

"No! I don't—I don't want to be pretty!"

"She's afraid," Dream Cloud volunteered.

"She doesn't need to be afraid of me!" The doctor laughed and went on.

But she was. Now that he had found out about her foot she would never be able to "rest her heart." From now on, she thought miserably, he might take a notion to operate on it, just any day.

The next morning, Dr. Lo appeared, friendly and cheerful as he always was, and instead of discussing her foot, he just told the girls they could go back to school.

Fragrant Jade wondered what her father would say if he knew that she had been in the hospital run by the foreign-devil doctor. She had not done it from choice. But she hoped her father would not make it an excuse for refusing to let her come back to school next term.

She told Bright Wisdom all about her stay in the hospital. "I'm afraid of the doctor," she confessed. "Do you think he does fearful things people say he does?"

"Of course not!" Bright Wisdom was amused. "Dr. Lo's a wonderful doctor. I'd trust him about anything."

Fragrant Jade only frowned.

"Didn't I ever tell you I'm going to be a nurse? I supposed you knew it. And after I get my training I'd like to come back and work here. I'd be lucky to work with Dr. Lo."

"You—a nurse?" Fragrant Jade tried to imagine her Big Sister a nurse, like Nurse Chi. Bright Wisdom was right about almost everything. But surely this was one place where she was mistaken.

CHAPTER FIVE

THROUH OCTOBER, one bright sunny day followed another. Nights were cool. Heavy farm carts unloaded in the yard at the Third Court huge heaps of cornstalks and *kaoliang* stalks. In the late afternoon, while one group of girls were getting supper, others carried a bundle of stalks to each room, and poking them under the brick bed, lighted them. The smoke floated out to join that of their neighbors in the village, who were occupied in the same task of warming their brick beds against the evening chill. The sun set every night in the soft haze made by the smoke from all their fires.

The red and gold leaves on trees and vines fell before the heavy late frosts. From near-by homes women and girls swarmed over the school grounds. With coarse bamboo rakes they frantically scratched together dried leaves, grass and twigs into baskets which they carried off on their backs to empty on their home fuel piles. Fragrant Jade paid no heed to their feverish activity. Busy with lessons and schoolgirl chatter, she felt none of the bustle of harvest which had accompanied every autumn of her life so far. She took no thought of the changing seasons, except as she added warmer clothing from her shelf in the dormitory: first, lined jackets and trousers, and then as needed, padded ones.

The school was just outside the South Gate. Girls from inside the city or from any of the near-by villages went home every night, as Fragrant Jade herself had done when she attended the West Market School. She was glad to be staying at a dormitory, where a person was never lonely. One of her favorite playmates was Boy—Boy with her frisky spotted puppy. They played at school, but Boy, who had no one at home to play with, wanted Fragrant Jade to go home from school to play with her. Finally one day she got permission from Miss Chang.

She and Boy ran all the way, and dashed into a courtyard which was much less neat than Fragrant Jade was used to. Both at her home and at school the courtyard was carefully swept every morning.

37

This one looked as though it had not been swept for a week. The three-room house on the north side of the court lacked paint, and its upper windows were stained and dirty. By the doorway sat an old man, absently holding a small bamboo cricket cage. Boy did not bow to this grandfather of hers, nor go to find her mother to bow and say, "I'm here," as a child coming from school ought to do. The little dog, Jumpy, was waiting to play, so the girls laughed and chased him and each other till they were breathless.

Fragrant Jade had not noticed when Boy's mother came out of the house and began to watch them. But when she sat down to get her breath, she found a round-faced, snub-nosed, pudgy little woman right beside her.

"You're the girl with the club foot," she remarked so bluntly that Fragrant Jade was taken aback. "Our child told about you when she came from school," she went on, plainly curious. She came closer, looking all the time so intently at the foot that Fragrant Jade squirmed, and drew it back an inch or two. She did not want to be impolite, but she wished she were somewhere else.

Boy's mother squatted beside the object of her interest, and pointing to it asked, "Do you have to keep it bound, inside of that shoe?"

Fragrant Jade glanced at Boy, who looked very uncomfortable. She was uncomfortable herself. She stood up.

"I guess I'll have to go back to school now," she suggested, hoping that Boy would not argue the point.

"Go slowly, go slowly," Boy answered in a meek little voice, following Fragrant Jade toward the gate.

"That foot doesn't seem to hinder her," Boy's mother was saying to no one in particular. "She surely moves fast."

Going to Boy's house to play had started out to be such fun! And then it had turned out not to be any fun at all.

Fragrant Jade had never been inside a city, and she wondered what shops looked like. In her home village of West Market there were no stores. There was only, on every tenth day, a market, when people came from all directions carrying whatever they had to sell, and meeting on the main road of the village, sold what they had, and bought what they wanted.

One morning Fragrant Jade asked Bright Wisdom, "Have you ever bought things from a store?"

"Lots of times."

"I never have, and I want to. We don't have shops in our village."

"I'll ask Miss Chang to let me take you into the city on this very Saturday afternoon for a shopping trip."

"I want to go, too," Dream Cloud said.

"Me, too!" Like-an-Orchid piped up.

"Do all your jobs before then," Bright Wisdom advised.

Saturday mornings there were classes as usual but the afternoon was a half-holiday. It was the busiest time of the week. The girls cleaned their rooms, washed their clothes, took baths, washed their hair, and did their mending.

During that week, Bright Wisdom's roommates took her advice. Every afternoon after school, they did one or another of the things they usually did on Saturday, so that when the half-holiday came, they were free.

Right after lunch, off they started. The road led past the hospital, through the big south city gate, along dusty alleys between courtyard walls. Fragrant Jade was surprised when they came to a big lotus pond inside the city. She had supposed cities were solidly houses.

After walking nearly two miles, they came out onto a wider street, and there, at last, were the shops. The four girls moved very, very slowly, looking first at one side and then at the other. The fronts of some of the shops were made of glass, instead of having paper windows. People could see the contents from the street: silver jewelry, or pens and paper, or cloth, or cakes, or grain. Even more interesting were places that were open to the street. The vegetable merchant had spread out cabbages, squash, onions, green and red peppers, turnips, egg plant, and many other vegetables, showing their pretty colors to the best advantage. The fruit shops were gaudy with golden tangerines, red-gold persimmons, purple grapes, and yellow and red apples and pears of several kinds.

Fragrant Jade needed to buy a piece of soap. The girls went to a "miscellaneous shop," where there were candles and matches, umbrellas, enamelled cups, wash basins, and a hundred other things.

How exciting it all was! The girls had passed several cross streets and made a turn or two, when they came to a big open space through which ran a small stream. Both banks were filled with the sort of outdoor buying and selling Fragrant Jade was accustomed to in her home village. Cloth peddlers held up one piece after another, yelling hoarsely what strong material it all was. At different booths one could buy every kind of food. One place smelled of fried cakes, another of steaming sweet potatoes, and farther on another of roasting

chestnuts. By the road, on patches of blue cloth spread on the ground, were peanuts, measured into tiny equal hillocks, each priced at two coppers. Sometimes, instead of being blue, the cloth was a dirty, coarse white one, or a gunny sack, and the wares were padlocks, or scissors, or rope, or toys, or brushes. Some of the merchants called out constantly what sounded like songs about what they had to sell. Like-an-Orchid spied a Punch and Judy show, but the other girls refused to wait while she looked at it. They led her on to see what else they could find.

Small boys dodged through the crowd that sauntered back and forth or ate at the booths. Catching sight of the four schoolgirls, several little fellows stopped to gawk at them.

"Look!" "A crippled girl student!" "A crooked-foot!"

Their shrill voices drew the attention of half a dozen others who came running. One began to mimic Fragrant Jade, jumping around on the side of his foot while he made faces and funny noises. On both sides grown-ups stopped to stare, too. Fragrant Jade's face burned, and tears came to her eyes.

Bright Wisdom had no thought of crying! She happened to have stopped by a cloth-seller whose foot rule lay on the ground beside him while he grinned appreciatively at small boys teasing a cripple.

"I'll borrow this a minute," Bright Wisdom said, grabbing up the ruler and starting after the mimic. "Little barbarians! You'll turn out bad!" she shouted at the boys. She was so big and strong and looked so determined to chastise anyone who dared to plague her companion, that the mischief-makers disappeared like magic, and even the grown-ups thought best not to be seen smiling.

But the trip was spoiled for Fragrant Jade. She wanted to hide, and cry. Must she always be made fun of? "Let's go home," she begged.

"Yes," Like-an-Orchid agreed, "let's do! I'm awfully tired!"

"All of us are worn out," Bright Wisdom said. "This market will be here whenever we want to come. We're foolish to try to see it all in one day."

On the way home she talked about Peking. "This city we're in is just a small one," she explained. "It hasn't more than fifteen or twenty thousand people. Peking must have a million or more. And you should see the shops! There are thousands of them, and you can buy anything in the world that you want. It's wonderful! You must all go there sometime."

Fragrant Jade thought she could scarcely hope ever to see the great capital city. How would she get such a chance? She thought this one she was in was wonderful enough. When she went home, she was going to tell her mother all about it.

The days were dry and cold and sunny, as late autumn and early winter days in North China usually are, and there was not much to mark one from the other. How fast they went by! Every six weeks there was an examination. The second six weeks were already past. Less than one-third of Fragrant Jade's precious term of school was left.

One afternoon it was cloudy, and the air felt damp. The next morning when the girls awoke, everything was covered with snow and big flakes were falling. At school, Teacher-mother Chao called the attention of her class to the beautiful crystals, and taught them a song about snow. All morning the snow fell fast until it lay four inches or more deep. Fragrant Jade had never seen so much snow before.

By noon the sky was clear, and the world lay fresh and clean. At lunch time no one talked of anything else.

Dream Cloud started it off. "Teacher Ho told us that in some places in her Beautiful Country, snow gets as much as six feet deep."

"Didn't she mean six inches?" one asked.

"She was only boasting," another remarked.

"But," another girl said, "she's been there and you haven't. Besides, she hasn't told us any lies, so why don't you believe this that she says?"

"But how could people live there? No one could go through it, and if you tried to walk on top you surely would sink in."

"I know the answer," Bright Wisdom said. "I asked Teacher Ho. She said they have machines that shovel the snow to each side leaving a passage through. She says it's like our roads out in the country, where the fields on each side are higher than the road. And she says they also have a way to walk on top of deep snow. She showed us a picture of the special shoes they wear, like tennis rackets."

"It might be!" the girls said, but they laughed at the funny notion.

After lunch the older girls made a snow man. Fragrant Jade had never seen that way of playing. At home, when there was even a little snow, everyone tried to stay indoors. "It's a foreign custom," she heard a big girl say, "but it's fun. The American children at their school over there have made a man twice as tall as ours. But ours is big enough."

They made mounds of snow over all the school grounds, and rolled balls for heads, and made black eyes by putting in coal balls. Everybody worked at it, and before afternoon classes began, half a dozen snow men sat about the yard, smiling in their silly fashion. The girls carried Mei-mei out to show her the unusual sight.

That afternoon, one of the old girls said, "Teacher-mother, isn't it time to begin to sing Christmas songs? Today, while the snow is on the ground, can't we sing about Good King Wencelas?"

They all seemed to know the song by heart. By the fourth or fifth stanza, the new girls were humming it, too. Then they sang "Here we come a-carolling," another long one which all the old girls knew. Fragrant Jade had never sung these songs. At West Market she had learned "Hark, the Herald Angels Sing," and "Away in a Manger." She was too bashful to ask for the ones she knew, but soon someone else chose them, and she could sing with the other girls.

"What is Christmas?" a new girl asked. "I never heard of it before."

So Teacher-mother Chao told her the story that Miss Wang had told many times to the little West Market children. Fragrant Jade thought it was even nicer than it had been the first time she heard it. She loved the Baby Jesus and his pretty mother, and the shepherds, and the Wise Men.

"It's several weeks till Christmas," the teacher-mother said, "but we'll sing some of the songs every day and plan how we want to celebrate."

All the old girls were full of ideas of what to do.

"Let's get a box right away to put coppers into, so we'll have enough corn meal to make a poor family really very happy," one said.

"I have a box," another said, and ran to get it.

"May we make little gifts for each other?" "I want to paint Christmas cards."

"Please, Teacher-mother, may we give a play?" "Let's learn our carols by heart so we can sing them in the night." They barely waited for each other to speak.

Every day after that, lessons were studied as fast as possible to save time for other activities. Getting ready for Christmas here was much more exciting than at West Market.

One morning, about a week before the happy day, Fragrant Jade was called out of class. "Your father has come for you. Your older brother is taking a bride soon. You have to go home to help your mother and be present at the wedding."

No Christmas at boarding school! Disappointed, Fragrant Jade ran out to greet her father, who was standing in front of the main building holding a donkey's rope. She stopped about four feet away from him, stood very straight with her feet together, and made a deep bow. "My father has come," she said.

"*Aye*, I've come to take you home."

"That's what they told me . . . Don't you think this is a lovely school?" She spoke proudly. Surely he would be able to see how perfect it was!

Without looking up at the building he grunted, and then said, "Let's go."

"I must get my things from the Third Court." There was tears in her eyes. She wanted him to like it! But she wasted no time. In a few minutes, without even telling her roommates good-by, she was down the road, out of sight of the school.

CHAPTER SIX

FRAGRANT JADE had put on all her winter jackets, one on top of the other, for the cold ride to West Market. She bounced along on top of the donkey, and her father drove it, running along behind in the narrows paths between the bare fields. She would have liked to tell him she was grateful for the good times he had allowed her to have at boarding school, but carrying on a conversation was impossible. And whenever they stopped to cross a ditch, somehow she could not get the sentence started.

She was really disappointed to miss Christmas at school, where there promised to be so much excitement, to come home where no one knew there was such a day. As she rode along, she planned that perhaps she could leave the wedding festivities long enough to go to the little church on Sunday morning to sing with the school children. That would be all she could do to keep Christmas this year.

Even so, a wedding is a wedding, and though this one came at the wrong time, still it would be fun, too. Little by little her spirits rose, so that when she came into sight of the big red gate of home, she called out to her father, and pointed, and was glad she was there again.

As she ran into the courtyard, the first thing she saw was a new two-room house on the east side, facing west. She knew without needing to be told that Big Brother and his bride would live there. She did not stop to look at it now.

Running in, she called, "Mother, here I am," and bowed deeply. She hurried into the inner room to give her grandfather his bow of greeting, and then she was ready to hear all the home news.

"As soon as you had gone to school, your father decided that I must have a girl to help with the work," her mother said, "so we are getting your brother a wife."

"Who is she?"

"She is the oldest daughter of a Li family at Pinetree Village. Old Liu the money lender arranged the match, so we suppose the Li family owe him money, and he's using this way to get some of it, by making

45

them give him her marriage portion. That makes us think the family is poor, but the girl herself may be all right. Old Liu says she's fifteen years old, good-looking and healthy, and can cook and sew perfectly, but of course he'd tell us she was wonderful even if she was an idiot."

"But, Mother! Couldn't you get some of our neighbors to ask their neighbors, and so find out a little more?"

"Naturally I did. So far we haven't heard anything bad about her. Anyway, it's settled now. We couldn't get out of it if we wanted to, no matter what we found out."

"When's the wedding?"

"In eight days. There's so much yet to be done, your father thought you ought to come home and help."

"Of course I ought."

"I haven't finished the bedding yet, so I think you can work first on that," Mrs. Chou said in a worried tone.

Fragrant Jade sewed up one side, then patted the cotton smooth in a new red comforter. When she had sewed up the other edges, she embroidered patterns on the square ends for the hard rectangular pillows.

The bride's two rooms looked bare, with only the built-in brick bed, and pine tables and stools, but they grew cheerier and more home-like when the new comforters and pillows were finished and folded and made into a neat scarlet pile on the brick bed. Fragrant Jade brushed the grass mat on the bed, dusted the furniture, and washed the four small square panes of glass set into the middle of the clean paper windows. While she worked, she wondered what her new sister-in-law would be like.

Two days before the wedding there was a market day. Grand-father stayed to watch the house, while Fragrant Jade went with her mother to buy fruit, vegetables, and meat for the wedding feast.

"My mother and brother and his wife and those three little children will get here any moment now," Mrs. Chou said as they hurried along the village street. Fragrant Jade did not need to be told that their entertainment was not worrying her mother. They would eat just the everyday food: cabbage, bean sprouts, and homemade salt vegetable with corn meal or millet porridge. It was only for the twenty or more neighbors who would eat with them on the wedding day that she had to buy extras: pork, and water chestnuts, persimmons, and pears, and tangerines, and some hard candy. She had planned every cent carefully, how to buy a wee bit of each expensive thing, and more of the cheaper things, to make a good showing with her money.

Each market day was sure to be interesting because it was sure to be different from every other. The main street of the village was full of people standing or squatting by their wares if they were selling, or walking here and there if they were buying. Fragrant Jade and her mother passed two men bargaining over a sleepy old ox, and near them a man with two pigs looking hopefully for a buyer. Next they came to the place where both sides of the street were full of open bags showing corn and millet and *kaoliang*. Mrs. Chou did not even look at these. She had grain at home. But she soon found what she wanted, and within half an hour, she and Fragrant Jade were starting home with their hands full of their little purchases.

As they came in sight of their gate, the grandmother and uncle's family were just arriving. Fragrant Jade could not remember when they had ever visited her home before, though they lived only a few miles away. Sometimes her uncle had stopped for a few minutes on his way to market or elsewhere on business, but she had seen her grandmother and aunt only on the old lady's birthdays when her mother had taken her to their home for a few hours. This was all according to custom. When a Chinese girl marries, she belongs to her husband's family and often sees almost nothing of her own parents for the rest of her life. On special occasions like weddings and funerals, however, the families get together.

Mrs. Chou's welcome to her "mother's family" was noisy and jolly. She and Fragrant Jade hurried to make tea for the guests, chilled by their long ride. The little cousins were all boys, called Little Baldy, Little Second, and Little Third. At first nobody had time to pay attention to them, but when all the grown-ups were sipping their tea, Fragrant Jade gave each of the children a piece of hard candy to suck. They were shy, but after a few minutes, Little Baldy began to follow her around while she refilled the teacups, and then Little Second toddled after. Only the baby, Little Third, still stared at her from his mother's lap.

How tongues chattered! Grandmother and Aunt had to be told everything that was known or guessed about the bride. They told the news from their village. Then they had to hear all about Fragrant Jade's school. Neither of them had ever been inside a school, but they had heard many tales, and she laughed merrily at the queer bits of gossip they had heard and believed about the "Jesus church," and the boarding school and hospital.

Fragrant Jade told about Teacher-mother Chao and her classmates, about her nice roommates and life in the Third Court. She told about

Boy and Jumpy. She told about the two-storied buildings, about the Americans who lived near by, with their blue-eyed, yellow-haired children some of whom she had seen. She told about the shopping trip she and her roommates had taken. She even told about the hospital, and the busy doctor and nurse. But she did not mention how strangers laughed at her crooked foot, or what Teacher Ho had said about making it straight. She intended that no matter what happened, she would not let the foreign doctor touch it, so why say anything at all about the subject?

The last busy days were gone before she knew it, and it was the wedding morning, cold and clear. All at the Chou house were up early and dressed themselves in bright new clothes. Fragrant Jade had a jacket and trousers of green calico, with a pattern of large pink and red flowers, and felt as gay as her clothes. Pinetree Village was so near that the bride in her red sedan chair might easily arrive before the morning was half gone. So the neighbors came early, and Fragrant Jade was busy helping her mother and father to welcome their guests and to serve them with tea as they stood about in the sunny courtyard.

At last there was a distant sound of wedding gongs and horns. What excitement! Second Brother got some boys to help him shoot off strings of little firecrackers outside the front gate, so the bride hearing them would know she was being welcomed. Fragrant Jade ran back and forth. She couldn't wait!

Though the chair seemed to come so slowly, it did at last arrive. There followed the ceremonial bowing to ancestors, to parents, to each other, and last to the guests—what the villagers had always known as a wedding ceremony. Fragrant Jade stood in the front row, her heart jumping, and her eyes busily seeing everything. Her brother looking white and stiff, and the bride entirely covered with red. Her dress was embroidered red satin. Her head was covered with ornaments of red and silver. She wore long tasselled earrings. Her face was covered with a red cloth.

A few minutes later, the bride was led into her new home and seated on the edge of the brick bed. Fragrant Jade squeezed through the crowd that followed her in, so that when her Big Brother uncovered his bride's face and saw it for the first time, she saw it as soon as he did.

She had not pictured a girl only a little older than Dream Cloud and not nearly so old as Bright Wisdom. The bride's smooth young round face was expressionless under thick powder and rouge. "This

is my new sister-in-law," Fragrant Jade told herself. It was hard to imagine that this strange girl would live in their house after this, where until today she herself had been the only daughter.

Mrs. Chou needed help in serving the feast. Fragrant Jade ran back and forth to the tables carrying dishes and food. She had only enough time to whisper to her mother, "I think she looks nice."

Her mother whispered back, "She looks healthy enough. Let's hope she has a good disposition."

Whenever Fragrant Jade could get a minute, she ran into her brother's new house to take another look at the bride, and to see how she was enduring the teasing of their guests and the neighbors' small boys. She showed she knew how a bride ought to behave. Motionless, she sat looking at the floor.

As soon as the guests had eaten, they went home. The family relaxed, and talked over the day's festivities. Everything had gone well, and they were pleased with the bride.

"Her feet are bound quite small," Fragrant Jade's grandmother remarked approvingly. "The family must not be too poor and ignorant."

It would not be polite to argue with her grandmother, but Fragrant Jade knew that the girls at school would think nothing of her grandmother's tiny feet because she was of the older generation, but they would consider her "poor and ignorant" herself for admiring tiny bound feet in a young girl, now that they were no longer in style. "Poor Sister-in-law!" Fragrant Jade thought. "She's probably suffered more to bind her feet than I have being a cripple. And all for nothing! For, certainly, I must talk Mother into having her unbind them. Teacher-mother says it's a bad old custom, and we must all help the country women to give it up, as those in the cities have."

Little Baldy and Little Second were tired and cross, so Fragrant Jade wheedled them into going out to the kitchen where she gave them some candy, and then sang them to sleep. It was evident that their mother seldom had such a good time as she was having today.

The next day, as soon as the relatives had gone home, Mrs. Chou took her new daughter-in-law for the customary calls on the neighbors. When they were all gone, Fragrant Jade suddenly remembered Christmas. She counted quickly on her fingers. The day was already past, and she had forgotten to go to the little church to sing. She would have to wait for another Christmas.

On the second day after the wedding, according to custom, the bride returned to her mother's home, taking with her the bridegroom to get acquainted with her family. The wedding was over.

"Has Father said anything about next term?" Fragrant Jade asked her mother anxiously, when she was getting ready to start back to school.

"We'll talk about that when you come home for New Year's."

"But, Mother!"

"I'm sure it's better to wait. But be careful not to displease him."

Although it was the first of January, there were still several weeks before the Chinese New Year. Tuition and board were paid through the last moon of the old year. She was sure of these weeks, but she had to go back to school without knowing whether these were the last of her days as a student.

CHAPTER SEVEN

REACHING THE SCHOOLROOM was like returning to a second home. Someone asked about the wedding, but nobody listened to Fragrant Jade's answer. Final examinations were only three weeks away.

"I'm so frightened," True Pearl shuddered.

The other girls laughed, and the teacher-mother said, "A girl who is a good scholar doesn't need to be afraid of term examinations."

"A girl . . . a scholar? A girl couldn't be a scholar, could she?" Fragrant Jade asked.

"She could make a start, couldn't she?" one of her classmates said. "She could grow into a scholar, couldn't she?"

"Of course," the teacher-mother answered, "just the same as a boy would."

No one else in the room seemed to doubt it. Anyway, Fragrant Jade thought, she was glad her seatmate was the head of the class. Making up lessons was easy with True Pearl beside her to tell her instantly every word she did not know.

Boy, as usual, was not worried about lessons. She had taken her tiger home. Fragrant Jade missed his yellow eyes peering at her every time she looked up. But, the next day, Boy appeared with a cricket cage about four inches square, made of slender reeds. It was the one Fragrant Jade had seen Boy's grandfather holding—the sort many old gentlemen carry to take their pet crickets for a walk.

"My grandfather's cricket died," Boy reported sadly, "so he let me borrow the cage, but I haven't any cricket to put into it." She kept it in her desk, but took it out at intervals all day and looked at it solemnly.

That evening at the Third Court there was great excitement. Li Nai-nai's cat had caught a small gray mouse, and was playing with it in the yard.

"Quick!" Fragrant Jade called. "Let's take it away from the cat. We can keep it in Boy's cricket cage."

They found a little box, and the next morning carried the mouse to school, where, to Boy's delight, they squeezed it into her cricket cage. Before the bell rang, she slipped into the schoolroom with the cage dangling by a string, and hid it in her desk without the teacher-mother seeing her.

Amused glances passed between the girls as Teacher-mother Chao, without knowing about Boy's new pet, went innocently on with the reviews. In arithmetic class, slate pencils tapped loudly all over the room. Occasionally Boy took a peek at the mouse, which sat most of the time quite motionless.

Then they reviewed history. One pupil after another told the stories they had learned. A big girl in the back was droning through something about one of the early kings of the Middle Kingdom, when suddenly there was a small grating sound. The mouse was chewing the reed on one side of his cage. Boy patted the under side of her desk to frighten him, while keeping her eyes fixed on the teacher-mother's face for fear she might hear something. The mouse stopped chewing, and the teacher-mother had not noticed anything.

Soon it was Boy's turn to recite. She stood up and began, but right away the mouse began, too. Poor Boy! She talked louder, but every time she took a breath, everyone could hear, "scrunch, scrunch, scrunch." Boy tried to talk faster as well as louder, but she could not think of enough to say so fast, so she said the same sentence over and over while she tried to think of some more. All the time the naughty mouse kept chewing the reeds. Finally, without really finishing, Boy sat down. Fragrant Jade was a little embarrassed too. After all, the cunning new pet had been her idea.

"I'm afraid the mouse will spoil your grandfather's cricket cage," the teacher-mother surprised them by saying. "Perhaps you'd better go to the school kitchen and beg some corn bread for it to eat instead. Then put it on your desk where we can all see it, and maybe it'll keep quiet." Was there ever anything that the teacher-mother did not know?

Boy almost ran to get the crumbs, she was so glad to get out of sight. Soon the mouse was eating happily away, and the history lesson was not interrupted any more.

One day about a week before school was out, Fragrant Jade met the American teacher whom they called by her Chinese name, Miss Ho. Fragrant Jade was always a little afraid of her. She made her nicest bow.

Miss Ho stopped. "The term is nearly over," she began abruptly, "and we've never got around to straightening that foot of yours."

"I . . . Oh, I . . ." Fragrant Jade was sorry now that she had never told the foreign teacher that it was her intention never to let the doctor operate on her foot.

"I'm afraid I've neglected you."

"I . . . I don't think the doctor could fix it," Fragrant Jade stammered, instead of saying once and for all, as she had planned, that he would never have a chance to try.

"When I asked him about it, he said he hadn't seen it, so he couldn't say definitely, but he supposed an operation was possible. You might stay and have it done during the holidays."

"No! Oh, no! My father wouldn't let me!" Fragrant Jade thought with horror how unsuitable it would be to tell Miss Ho what her father thought about the "foreign-devil doctor."

"I suppose not. You girls can't stand missing Chinese New Year's at home. But you ought to consider how nice it would be to have a straight foot like other people."

When Fragrant Jade only continued to shake her head, Miss Ho walked on. Fragrant Jade was repeating to herself bitterly the teacher's words, "You ought to consider how nice it would be . . ." What did Miss Ho know about how nice it would be? She had never been laughed at. Not to limp at every step? To enjoy playing games? During the recent days Fragrant Jade had been taunted more often than before by such dreams, but she knew they were only dreams, and that they would not come true. The mere thought of what that American doctor might do made her heart tight inside her body. The difficult problem she really hoped to find a solution for was how to get her father to let her come back to school. Talking about a straight foot was a pure waste of time.

As the vacation time drew nearer, her friends counted the hours until they could go home. Fragrant Jade walked about from one courtyard to another, looking lovingly at the buildings. She could see in her imagination how the school had appeared when she first came, bright with red and yellow flowers, and how it had looked later, too, when cosmos and asters had changed the prevailing shades to rose and lavender. Now the only color was the green of the evergreens, but the place was still beautiful to her.

Bright Wisdom went home the very afternoon school was out. When she had gone, Fragrant Jade packed what she thought Like-an-Orchid's mother would want her to take for the holidays. The little girl was going as far as Peking with Dream Cloud on the seven o'clock train in the morning.

Before daylight, all the Third Court girls were up, cooking and eating breakfast, putting the articles they wanted to take into the centers of the comforters under which they had slept, and rolling them into bulky, awkward bundles to carry home, while at the same time running to and fro to shout farewell messages to friends in other rooms. Those who were not going on the train went along and helped to fill the station platform with girls and baggage.

After the jolly noise and confusion of getting the others off, the deserted cold room Fragrant Jade came back to was all the more depressing. Now it was time to pack her own things, all of them. It was not hard to do, but when she had finished, and looked again to be sure she had not left anything, her eyes filled with tears. Her drawer in the cupboard, and her shelf in the corner were both sickeningly empty of any sign that she had ever been there.

Second Brother came for Fragrant Jade, and he hired donkeys for True Pearl and the Chen sisters to travel with them. The January sun shone brightly, and there was no wind. As they bounced along, the girls kept trying to make their stubborn little beasts trot side by side, so they could talk to each other. Their thoughts ran ahead homeward. It was the twenty-second day of the last moon of the old year, and so the next day would be an important one in the holiday celebrations. Clear Virtue mentioned it.

"I'm glad we'll get home in time to say good-by to the kitchen god before he goes to heaven."

"I'll be glad to eat all the date pudding I want, anyway," True Pearl agreed.

"I'll get acquainted with my new sister-in-law," Fragrant Jade said proudly.

"Let's hope she won't be jealous of you," Glorious Virtue commented.

"Jealous?"

"Where have you been all these years, innocent? Don't you know that most sisters-in-law are jealous? She knows perfectly well that your mother likes you better than she does her."

"My mother could never be an unkind mother-in-law. She'll like us both." Fragrant Jade felt sure that what she said was true, but her friend's remark bothered her.

When Fragrant Jade reached her own home, she found her farmer father and older brother in their winter leisure gambling contentedly with her mother in the warm room, while her sister-in-law prepared the meal. They stopped their game to hear her tell about her trip home, and about the last weeks of school. Of them all, only Sister-in-law paid no attention. She acted as though she did not know any-one had come, and when she served the meal, she put Fragrant Jade's bowl barely within her reach.

"What can I have done to displease her?" Fragrant Jade wondered.

The next morning, Mrs. Chou let Fragrant Jade help her make date pudding. Its fragrance filled the house as it steamed all day over the big iron kettle. Farmer Chou made a small horse of dried grass.

In the evening he took from the wall above the stove the faded red picture of the kitchen god, and placed it on the center table with the grass horse, a bit of grass for the horse to eat on its journey and a cup of water for it to drink. Mrs. Chou melted a piece of malt candy to rub on the kitchen god's mouth. A generous portion of date pudding was set before him.

Then, beginning with the grandfather, from the oldest to the youngest, each member of the family knelt and bowed to the floor before him three times, asking him please to be a kind god and report only good things of their household when he arrived in heaven.

After that, Mr. Chou reverently burned the picture, the little horse, and the hay, while all the others kept bowing to the floor and pleading with the kitchen god to forget everything wrong they had done.

Fragrant Jade had done this every year, all her life. When the ceremony was over, she could have all the date pudding she could eat. She loved date pudding!

The short winter days flew by. Fragrant Jade did whatever her mother assigned her. The house had to be cleaned thoroughly, and a great deal of cooking had to be done, all the cakes and meat dishes they could afford to be put carefully away in a cold place for use in the holidays.

Along with her other duties, Sister-in-law was making new cloth shoes for Fragrant Jade, and they must be finished before New Year's Day, because it is considered unlucky to wear shoes made in the first month of the new year.

"I'm afraid you won't get them done," Mrs. Chou worried, "and I can't understand why. You can sew so well and so fast, and there's nothing hard about making a couple of pairs of shoes. Yet look at them! Not much more than started!" She went to the next room.

"Shoes for a cripple!" Sister-in-law muttered. Fragrant Jade's face grew hot, and she could not see for tears. What had she done to deserve this?

Yet that was only one of dozens of little unkindnesses with which every day was filled. Sister-in-law never spoke to Fragrant Jade, but always acted as if she were as invisible as the air. Her comments were made to herself in an audible undertone. Fragrant Jade did not want to tell her mother. Mrs. Chou was very mild-tempered, but she would be angry and might punish Sister-in-law. Fragrant Jade could not get over the idea that the girl was a guest in their house with special privileges. Besides, she was no tattle-tale, to run to her mother. Yet in her memory New Year's time was one of jolly chatter, whereas this year there were long silences.

Mrs. Chou noticed it, too. "How quiet you girls are! Neither of you seems to say anything to the other. If the idea weren't so silly, I could almost suspect you didn't like each other."

Fragrant Jade pretended that her only reason for keeping so still was anxiety over whether she could go back to school. It seemed to her that the topic never left her thoughts. She had asked her mother about it as soon as she got home.

"We'll wait till it's nearly time for you to go back," Mrs. Chou had decreed, "and then I'll ask your father."

But waiting was hard.

Farmer Chou and his sons spent the last day of the old year collecting debts owing to them, and paying their accounts. They were not so rushed but that they could stop and pass the time of day with their friends. Mrs. Chou had already bought plenty of incense, new gate gods, a new kitchen god and two pictures of the god of wealth, besides lacy red paper to put over the door, and lucky mottoes to paste opposite the door. Her two sons had bought a supply of firecrackers. The house was cleaned, the extra cooking was done. They were ready for New Year's.

As evening came on, they began to make dumplings. Fragrant Jade loved to help chop the vegetables and meat for filling, and later to pinch together the edges of the tiny circles of dough. Ever since she was a tiny girl, she remembered this as the jolliest part of the New Year. She and her mother had always talked about all kinds of silly things and laughed about everything. But Sister-in-law said nothing all evening, no matter how pleasantly Mrs. Chou spoke to her, until finally Fragrant Jade and her mother worked in silence, too.

Toward midnight the men came home. They pasted up the pictures of the new gods: the gate gods, the kitchen god, and the god of wealth. No one thought of going to bed. When the new year came in, they knelt and bowed their heads to the ground in reverence to their ancestors. Then the younger members of the family knelt to the older ones. First they all did homage to the grandfather, then the children to their parents, and finally Fragrant Jade knocked her head on the floor before her sister-in-law. At just the right time the dumplings were ready, and were at once presented to the ancestors and the gods, and then the family settled down to stuff themselves with all they wanted. Second Brother kept running out between bowls of dumplings to shoot off giant firecrackers. All the neighbors were doing the same things they were doing, and with all the excitement on hand, the dogs near and far never got a chance to stop barking.

On the first day of the new year, according to custom, the men went to see their near neighbors. Mr. Chou and his sons went calling, but the old grandfather stayed at home. Almost all day there was at least one friend visiting with him, and listening to him as he told stories of old times. The girls poured tea, and kept the men supplied with little cakes and watermelon seeds.

Fragrant Jade planned to stay up the second night too, as all the grown-ups did, but she fell asleep. At midnight, the noise of the family welcoming the god of wealth woke her. All the doors were open to give him easy entrance. In front of his picture sat a dish with five or six boiled eggs, and saucers with bits of other dainty food. They shot off many firecrackers to call his attention to their house. Farmer Chou burned the god's picture, and the men of the family all bowed to the floor. They hoped it would be a lucky year, and that the crops would be good.

After that, every day the whole family wore their good clothes and ate better food than usual. They received callers and visited their friends. On the fifth day of the new year, according to custom, Sister-in-law's brother, representing his parents, came from Pinetree Village to inquire after her welfare. He brought gifts that were considered appropriate—cakes and meat dumplings. Mrs. Chou sent Fragrant Jade to carry tea to Sister-in-law and her brother.

When Fragrant Jade reached the door of Big Brother's house, she heard Sister-in-law's voice complaining, "She's stuck up because she can read. She thinks because she's been to school she's better than people with two straight feet."

Fragrant Jade gasped. She wanted to turn back. But she rattled the door and went in. With burning cheeks and trembling fingers she served the tea, as her mother expected her to do, and then she hurried away. She was angry and hurt—disturbed as she could not remember ever having been before. The words kept coming back to her:

"She's stuck up, because she can read. She thinks she's better than people with two straight feet." She kept thinking of answers that she ought to make. Sister-in-law wasn't fair!

The fifteenth of the new moon is the Feast of Lanterns, the day to make *yuan hsiao*. Fragrant Jade had often tried, but hers were always a sticky mess. Sister-in-law could make them both quickly and successfully. She made little balls of nuts and dates and black sugar, then rolled them in rice flour. Then putting them into a sieve, she cooked them a moment in boiling water, rolled them again in rice flour, and so on.

"Look Mother, how clever Sister-in-law is!"

"Yes, she can make nearly as many things, and make them nearly as well as I can," said Mrs. Chou generously. "She's a remarkably good cook for her age."

"*Pu kan tang!* I dare not think so," her daughter-in-law said politely, but high as the praise was, she did not smile.

After Mr. Chou had had all the *yuan hsiao* he wanted, his wife remarked calmly, "Day after tomorrow is the day for our daughter to go back to school."

Fragrant Jade's heart seemed to stand still.

"What! Talking about school again!" he shouted angrily.

"She is of no use to you in the spring planting. Now that we have such a clever daughter-in-law, I don't need her in the house. She's barely fourteen, too young to marry. She really might just as well spend her time at school."

He turned toward Fragrant Jade. "What about the foreign-devil doctor?"

"Oh, nothing, Father . . . he . . . he . . . doesn't . . . he hasn't seen my foot."

Mr. Chou grunted.

Fragrant Jade did not know what best to say.

In her mother's hand were the little examination booklets she had brought home. Now, without waiting for her husband to ask any more questions, Mrs. Chou handed the little books to him. "Daughter," she said, "read your grades aloud for your father."

Fragrant Jade picked them up one by one, and though she knew he did not know how to read Arabic numbers, she pointed to each as she read: "Reading 92. Memory words 96. Arithmetic 97. Composition 90. Teacher-mother said I stood second in the class, Father. Only True Pearl got better grades, and nobody in the world could ever beat her!"

Her father said nothing. From his pocket he took an unhemmed square of cloth he used as a handkerchief, and tapping the examination books into a neat pile, he put them diagonally in the middle of the handkerchief and folded them into a tidy little parcel.

Fragrant Jade watched him breathlessly. What did he mean by that?

After he had tucked in the corner of the cloth to tighten the little bundle, he finally grumbled, "I suppose she might as well go back again."

As Fragrant Jade bowed deeply, saying, "Thank you, Father," she caught her mother's smile. Because she was a cripple she had never learned to hop around to express how happy she felt. But her heart was not hampered, as her body was, by a crooked foot. And her heart was **dancing.**

CHAPTER EIGHT

SPRING CAME, and one morning Boy arrived at school, her eyes sparkling, while she carried carefully a coarse rice bowl full of water.

"Pollywogs!" she called, spying Fragrant Jade by the schoolroom door.

"Where did you get them?"

"In the moat. And there are millions more! Let's ask the teacher-mother if we can raise them till they're frogs."

Teacher and students took up the project with enthusiasm. The Wu girl brought from home a green crock about a foot across, and Boy volunteered to catch enough pollywogs to fill it. The bank of the moat was soon full of her classmates watching and giving advice. The crockful of pollywogs was triumphantly established on a stool in a corner of the room, with the hope that they would hurry and grow.

Boy had another idea, and one day three small fish joined the pollywogs in the crock. "When they get big," Boy announced, "I'm going to cook and eat them."

At recess someone discovered that the fish thought the pollywogs were there for them to eat. A fish would swallow one, and when it wriggled, he would spit it out, and it would go swimming off quite unabashed by having just been eaten. The whole class watched entranced.

It was while Fragrant Jade was so occupied that she heard a call, "Fragrant Jade! Teacher Ho wants you to come to her office. You'd better get there fast. She doesn't like to wait."

Quickly Fragrant Jade ran through the courts looking for a friend to go with her. She spied Bright Wisdom. "Teacher Ho wants to see me, and I'm afraid to go alone."

"Come on! She won't hurt you."

Miss Ho welcomed them with, "I'm glad you came too, Bright Wisdom, because you can help Fragrant Jade remember all the things I'm going to tell her. This morning Dr. Lo brought word that she can have her foot straightened in Peking day after tomorrow."

Fragrant Jade had a sudden queer feeling inside her. Before she could object, Miss Ho was telling all about it, talking very fast, as she always did.

"A German doctor, famous for bone surgery, has come to lecture for a month at the Peking Union Medical College Hospital, and he'll be operating on a lot of different kinds of cases. Dr. Lo was there at the hospital for something and they asked him if he knew any people who needed such operations. When he saw 'club foot' on the list he thought of Fragrant Jade. You see, there's no charge for anything because the visiting surgeon will be using the operations to show the student doctors how. Imagine getting your foot straightened free, and by the man who is probably the best in the world at that particular thing!"

Fragrant Jade was not sure she understood it all, but she was sure that she did not like the idea. She interrupted Miss Ho's enthusiastic remarks with, "I don't want to!"

"Don't want to!"

"I'm never going to let a doctor touch it."

Miss Ho gazed at her in unbelief. "What? 'Never going to . . .' Do you mean to say you choose to keep such a handicap when you can get rid of it? Would you turn down a chance like this, and then when you're a young lady and graduate from school, would you plan to go limping across the platform to get your diploma?"

Fragrant Jade squirmed. She had not thought that far ahead. Such a situation would be embarrassing.

"Oh, I think she'll have it straightened," Bright Wisdom said in her Big Sister voice.

"I'll get it done when I'm in high school," Fragrant Jade offered. "My father won't let me now."

"Your father . . . " Bright Wisdom began. "He doesn't know . . ."

"He's already given permission," Miss Ho said, dismissing that objection as though she had answered it. "All parents who send their daughters here put them in Dr. Lo's care."

Yes, Fragrant Jade remembered the Wu girl, the rich girl whom the teacher-mother would have permitted to go home and stay there, "if she was unwilling to do what the doctor thought best."

"But I don't think he . . . he doesn't like the foreign doctor." She could not tell Miss Ho about her father, how hard it was to persuade him to let her come to school, and how he asked about the doctor so sternly. "I think he doesn't know . . . "

"If he doesn't know, he soon will," Miss Ho said confidently. "He has given the school the responsibility of looking after your health, but for a special thing like this, we send a letter to the parent. If he doesn't like it, all he has to do is come and stop it."

"A letter?" Fragrant Jade knew only one way for a letter to go to West Market. First it went to the county seat, to a grain shop that was used as a post office there. Then if anybody at the county seat was going to West Market on an errand, he would get the mail and carry it along. It would get there sometime, surely, but not soon. Anyway, her father could not read, and he might easily put off asking any one to read it to him for a month or two. There was no likelihood of his coming to stop the proceedings.

"Yes," Miss Ho went on, "as soon as we heard about it we sent a man on a bicycle out to your home with a letter to explain about it and a blank to sign. The man ought to be back by noon. Then this afternoon Dr. Lo will look at your foot to be sure it's what the hospital wants. You take her to see him, Bright Wisdom."

Show her foot to Dr. Lo? That was the thing she had said over and over she would never do. She could not swallow back the tears. "I don't want to," she wailed.

But the interview was over. Bright Wisdom was leading the way toward the door. "I'll take care of it," she promised Miss Ho.

Fragrant Jade's head was whirling with jumbled and conflicting impressions. She had said she would never let a doctor touch her foot. She was afraid of the doctor—of all doctors—of Dr. Lo, and of this even stranger German in Peking. What might they not decide to do to her! And her father? Surely he would be angry when he heard that the "foreign-devil doctor" was making a definite proposal to try to straighten her foot. She must get out of the scheme, and right away!

Bright Wisdom chatted cheerfully all the way till they separated to go to their own classrooms. Fragrant Jade had nothing to say. She went in and sat down beside True Pearl. She had never felt so small, so helpless. Her mind would not function. She gave up trying to make it learn her lessons. The fear that seemed to have taken complete charge of her body made her stupid. At noon, she went and sat in the corner of the yard, numb. Lunch was not worth going after. When the bell rang for afternoon classes, True Pearl found her huddled there.

"What are you doing?"

"Nothing."

"What's the matter?" Clear Virtue and Bright Virtue were joining them. She might as well tell them.

"I have to go to see the foreign doctor this afternoon."

"That's nothing!" True Pearl laughed. "I thought from the glum face that something awful had happened."

"It is awful! He wants to take me to Peking and operate on my foot." Tears kept running down her face.

"You mean he's going to straighten it?" the Chen girls chorused. "I think that's wonderful!"

In fact, all three were so well pleased with the idea that they called their classmates to tell them, and soon they were the center of an excited crowd, all rejoicing that Fragrant Jade was to have an operation. They asked dozens of questions, and when, along with the answers, she protested, "My father hasn't said I could and I haven't said I would, either," they refused to listen, hearing only what they chose to hear.

They carried the topic with them to the classroom, and the teacher-mother agreed that this was a wonderful chance. Fragrant Jade endured most of their enthusiasm in silence, but when the Wu girl made a remark, she retorted rudely, "You don't know anything about it. You never had an operation."

"She hasn't a club foot, either," the teacher-mother answered mildly.

The room was full of excitement all afternoon, though little more was said about its cause. At playtime, Bright Wisdom came and took Fragrant Jade to the hospital. Half a dozen other girls were going for other reasons. Fragrant Jade let them do the talking. She was trying to decide what she could say to the doctor. Every excuse she thought of seemed inadequate, but she was sure she must stick to one thing—that she was not going to Peking and that she did not want an operation, no matter what anyone said.

Nurse Chi met them at the door. She seemed to be waiting for Fragrant Jade and Bright Wisdom, and led them right into a small room with some tables, stools, and cupboards. She went out and returned immediately with Dr. Lo.

He greeted her so pleasantly that she hated to say he could not look at her foot because she was not going to do anything about it. Nurse Chi took off her shoe and short, white cotton stocking.

"Um . . ." the doctor said. It was embarrassing to have him looking so intently at the one part of her of which she was most ashamed. After a little he added, "That'll be all right."

"But! . . . but!" This was already going too far. She must tell him now.

"Yes?"

"I'm not going to have an operation . . . my father won't let me."

"That's all right! But perhaps you haven't heard. We sent a man out to West Market to get his permission. You don't need to worry about what the home folks think. Your father wasn't at home, but your grandfather put his thumbprint on the statement. That's a generation better."

"But . . ." She would have said that her grandfather never made the decisions at their house. But he had made this one, and decided the wrong way! "I'm not going to, even if he says I can."

"Because?"

"It'll hurt!" The minute she said it, Fragrant Jade remembered the Wu girl, whom she did not like. She changed to, "I just don't want to do it."

"Perhaps the thought of an operation does frighten you," Dr. Lo said kindly. "That's natural, and the main reason for it is that you don't know what you're getting into. But you mustn't let that loom too big in your eyes, because there are other things that ought to balance against it. For instance, aren't there a lot of disadvantages in having a club foot? Don't people make fun of you sometimes?"

Fragrant Jade could almost believe those clear brown eyes of his had actually seen her classmates mimicking her, he seemed so sure. "Yes," she conceded.

"And that's mighty hard to stand. So one of the things you have to think about is the possibility that people will do that the rest of your life, or, ... or, you can avoid that unpleasantness by doing something hard that won't last very long. That oughtn't to be a very difficult choice to make. Is it?"

"She hates to be laughed at," Bright Wisdom answered for her.

"But that's not all. You might even be able to get used to people's rudeness. But I'm sure that sometimes you get left out of doing something you'd like to do. Isn't that so? And wouldn't it be nice to think that for the rest of your life you wouldn't be hampered that way?"

Fragrant Jade only nodded. She could see where all this was leading. The doctor would talk her into agreeing to have the operation, and she did not want to!

He might have read her mind, for he went on, "I don't want to talk you into something. But it wouldn't be fair if, knowing as much as I do about it, I should neglect to put all the facts before you. You're a big girl. It's your foot, and your decision, but the rest of us know something about these things, and we have to give you the best advice we can."

She was putting on her shoe and stocking again. The tears kept dripping dismally off the end of her nose. "I don't want to . . . . . I don't want to . . . " she muttered.

"Once it's over, you'll always be glad." The doctor's voice was sympathetic. "You'll soon forget whatever discomforts there were, and it'll be fun to be free from this handicap. I wonder if you can imagine how much fun! Think about that now, instead of what you'll be doing for the next few weeks. The rest of your life is much longer and more important, too, isn't it?"

Again Fragrant Jade could only nod her head. What he said was so reasonable! She had no answer, and yet she did not want to do it!

Her shoe was on. She was ready to go.

"Well, how about it?"

"I don't want to!"

"That's right," the doctor answered, "you don't want to, but you'll do it because you think it's a good thing to get done, once's it's over. Is that what you mean?"

Fragrant Jade paused. Through her mind raced the things Dr. Lo had been saying, mixed with jumbled pictures of unpleasant incidents ever since she could remember. If the future need not be like that . . . . For how long, in the back of her mind, had been growing the wish for a straight foot! Maybe the famous doctor could straighten it . . . . Surely she could stand whatever pain was necessary for such a reward.

Finally she nodded her head.

"Good girl!" Nurse Chi praised her. "Now that you've made up your mind it'll be lots easier. It won't take many days. And you'll be glad always—all the rest of your life."

Fragrant Jade slipped her hand into Bright Wisdom's, and together they started back to school. She was not altogether happy. How was she ever going to endure what she had undertaken to do? But neither had it seemed possible to refuse to try what could make life so different.

The next morning she found that sometime in the night her attitude toward the operation had changed a little. She was not quite so frightened. One other thing had also occurred to her. She had made the decision as Dr. Lo had urged her to do, thinking of her own future. She had forgotten her father. Her grandfather's consent was all the hospital needed, but Fragrant Jade had no reason to suppose that her father had changed his mind. If she went to Peking and had an operation . . . ? What was he likely to say, she could only wonder.

Dr. Lo made the arrangements for her travel. Fragrant Jade was to go to Peking with Miss Ho at noon. She could not swallow any lunch, and her fingers trembled as she buttoned her clean blue school uniform. All the Third Court and many of her fourth year classmates went to the station with her. She held tightly to Bright Wisdom's hand. How she hated to leave her!

The train came chugging into the station. "Good-by! Good-by!" the girls called. "*I lu p'ing an!* A journey of peace!" They ran along the platform and waved when the train started. But they were soon left behind.

This was Fragrant Jade's first trip on a train, and though she would have enjoyed it more with Bright Wisdom, even with Miss Ho it was fun to see the trees and fields go rushing by. The car was crowded. How could so many people have business in Peking?

In a short time they arrived at a huge station where everyone ran in different directions and yelled as loudly as possible. Fragrant Jade had not seen half of it before she and Teacher Ho had come through a city gate and were inside Peking.

"We are too early for our appointment at the hospital," Miss Ho said, "and we don't want to sit and think about our own affairs. How would you like to go up on the city wall and look over the city?"

Fragrant Jade agreed that was a good idea, so they climbed a long incline to the top of a wide high wall, and all the great city lay spread before them. Miss Ho had been there before, and explained the shape of the city and told the names of the buildings whose roofs showed above the treetops.

"I never saw so many trees," said Fragrant Jade. They stretched as far as she could see. Miss Ho pointed out the yellow roofs of the Forbidden City, where the Emperor used to live, and she described the great courtyards. The Coal Hill showed clearly. After a while they looked south into the Chinese City. The streets below were crowded with people going in and out of the shops. It seemed a little impolite to look down into other people's courtyards and see the children playing and the mothers working in their yards. As far as they could see were buildings and people.

"There are many, many shops out there," Miss Ho said. "All kinds of things are for sale. It's a very busy place." Fragrant Jade

remembered how Bright Wisdom had said she might someday see the thousands of shops in Peking.

Farther to the south she saw the blue tile roof of the Temple of Heaven. Miss Ho explained, "It's very beautiul, something for all Chinese to feel proud of. Whenever you see it, you must remember that even from the most ancient times your ancestors recognized that Heaven was above all their gods."

They walked on the wall and talked for a half an hour or more. Fragrant Jade wondered why she had ever been afraid of Teacher Ho. The longer they talked, the less she noticed that Miss Ho had blue eyes and big feet and odd foreign clothes.

When they came down from the wall, they went north through streets full of interesting sights and people, and for the first time Fragrant Jade felt the queer jumpy feeling of being pulled in a ricksha. The ricksha puller saw nothing odd about it, and they rushed along smooth, wide streets between big buildings two or three stories high. The Peking Union Medical College Hospital looked like other Chinese buildings except that it was so big, with such fresh green tile roof.

Inside, long halls stretched far away, and up and down these hurried people dressed in white. Fragrant Jade felt very small in such big halls, but Miss Ho seemed not to mind.

"You will always remember this interesting day," she said. "I am sure you have seen more new things than on any other one day in your life, and there are many yet to see."

While they waited in a big room, Miss Ho showed Fragrant Jade the electric light, the electric fan, and the water-that-comes-by-itself. "Remember everything you see. Hardly any of your schoolmates have ever seen these things, and you must tell us all about them when you come back. Hardly anyone in school has ever had even a minor operation, either, so when they give you the medicine to put you to sleep, remember all about it so you can tell us. We shall all want to know what it feels like."

Fragrant Jade promised to try. A nurse came for her. There was no more time to talk. She was going to have to go by herself.

"Good-by," Miss Ho said cheerfully, "don't be afraid of anybody. They are all very clever people, but they are kind, too, and will not hurt you more than is necessary. Of course it will hurt, but don't think about that. Think about how happy you'll be to walk with a straight foot like other girls." She smiled and walked away.

Fragrant Jade felt a little afraid, but she was at the same time interested in where she went and what she saw. The big hospital turned out to be not so different from the little one where she had been with Dream Cloud. The ward had eight beds in it, all full of girls, and they were soon getting acquainted, asking her name, and where she had come from, and what she had come for. The doctors were like Dr. Lo, and nurses came and went, doing the sort of things Nurse Chi did.

After supper, Fragrant Jade began to think about the girls back at school having evening study hall and then evening prayers. She covered her head with the sheet and sang softly to herself "In Heavenly Love Abiding," the hymn they all liked best. She pretended she was singing with the others. She forgot her new neighbors, comforted by the words of the song.

"Sing some more! Uncover your head so we can hear!" the other children called after the first stanza. It was an easy thing to do for them. So she sang another of the many hymns she knew by heart, and then another, till she was really too sleepy to sing any more.

The next morning Fragrant Jade tried to obey Miss Ho and remember everything she did and saw, so she could report it to her schoolmates. The most frightening time was what she had said she would always avoid. So when she guessed that they were going to put her to sleep, she tried to fight against it. The nurse laughed and said, "All right. Blow it away." She blew as hard as she could, and that was the last she knew, until, waking up, she thought how tired she was, and that she would just sleep a little more.

She could not see her foot hidden in a big white plaster. The nurses said it was as straight as anybody's, and she need never walk on the side of it again. It was hard to believe. As Bright Wisdom, and Nurse Chi, and Dr. Lo, and all the rest had promised, she was glad —and more thrillingly glad every day.

There was only one worry. What would her father say?

CHAPTER NINE

Dr. lo himself came to take Fragrant Jade back to school. He took her directly to her classroom and he had her sit on the teacher-mother's desk, plaster cast and all. Her schoolmates came crowding in to ask about her experiences in the big Peking hospital. Dr. Lo left her there a while, and then came back and took her to his hospital to stay until the plaster cast could be removed from her foot.

Each afternoon True Pearl came to explain that day's lessons. Other girls ran in to tell the school news. The rest of the time Fragrant Jade studied hard to catch up with her class. Every morning she asked Dr. Lo when he would take off the plaster cast, and every day his brown eyes twinkled and he answered, "Not today."

But one morning he surprised her by saying before she asked, "We're ready to take off your cast."

"Today?" she asked excitedly.

"Right now! It'll be more interesting for you than when your foot was actually being straightened. That's the trouble with an operation. The person most affected is seldom in a condition to enjoy it."

"Enjoy it! Do you mean there are people who enjoy operations?"

"Perhaps 'enjoy' isn't the exact word, but I admit there's great satisfaction in removing harmful growths, and I like to fix up people's broken bones for them, too."

While his hands were busy cutting away the plaster cast, he talked about a doctor's work, and how he used many instruments and methods to relieve pain.

"I've always been afraid of doctors with their knives and things," Fragrant Jade confessed. "I thought they didn't care if it hurt. I didn't know their idea was to keep people from having to be hurt."

"Well, then, you've learned something, besides getting a better looking foot. Take a look at what the 'doctors with their knives and things' have done for you."

Fragrant Jade propped herself on her elbows and looking down at her own feet, saw for the first time in her life two straight ones. She

took a deep breath. "Straight! Both of 'em! And it just hurt a little. It wasn't ever too bad to stand. I wonder why I was so scared."

Briefly, but clearly Dr. Lo explained why she must keep her foot held straight, and how she could do it. He told her how tired she would get, but how important her part was. "It won't be easy, but you must break your old habit of standing on the side of your foot. If you should walk the way you did before, the whole operation will be a failure. You'll have new leather shoes that'll be uncomfortable because they're so stiff, but they'll help to remind you."

Fragrant Jade was sure she could manage. Anything would be easy now. Just then Dr. Lo was called away to another patient, and suddenly she realized that she had forgotten to thank him.

Some days later, Fragrant Jade returned to school. All her schoolmates, large and small, wanted to see her straight foot, as though it was something new she had bought in Peking. The homemade cloth shoes she had formerly worn had been made with soft cloth soles. The new leather shoes were stiff and heavy, and not only made her tired, but they made her so awkward that she had to learn to walk again. When the muscles were so weary that they actually hurt, she set her teeth together, and compelled her foot to stand straight. Dr. Lo was never going to have reason to scold her for having spoiled what the German doctor had done so well.

A hundred times a day she felt her heart light within her. But sometimes she wondered what her father was going to say. How could he fail to be pleased when he had seen her foot? Then she remembered the day when she had called his attention to her school buildings, and how unimpressed he had been with what she thought was so beautiful. He had never actually forbidden her to get a straight foot, so she had not exactly disobeyed him. Besides, her grandfather had given his consent. Perhaps, since it had all turned out so well . . . perhaps her father might even be glad. The important thing was to think of something special to do for him to win his favor so that he would not be angry, and so that he would let her come back to school. What could she do that would please him? No matter how hard it was, she would try. Surely it would have to be something very, very difficult to be worth such a prize! She could not think of a thing.

Fragrant Jade, remembering how her sister-in-law had acted at New Year's time, told Bright Wisdom about it.

"Jealous daughters-in-law are awfully common, I'm afraid," Big

Sister said. "You must keep your mother happy, and you, being her own daughter, care more about that than your sister-in-law does. So you'll be the one who has to give in to keep the peace. I think the only solution is never to tattle, or say anything unkind to her no matter what she does. You know the proverb, 'One hand can't clap out a noise'. It takes two to make a quarrel. You won't have to be patient with her very long. It'll be only during vacation. What if you had to stay at home all the time, and couldn't get away from her?"

"Oh, but I must get away!" Fragrant Jade gasped.

"Of course," Bright Wisdom remarked calmly, "you'll be here at school."

Fragrant Jade only wished she could be sure. How could she live if she was not allowed to come back to school?

Meanwhile, plans for Bright Wisdom's commencement were in the air. Fragrant Jade had never seen anybody's commencement. When late in June, the day came, the three roommates helped Bright Wisdom dress in her long light blue garment. She pinned up her heavy braids into two knots that changed her into a young lady. Their Big Sister was no longer a schoolgirl.

The celebration was held in the big hall at the boys' school, borrowed for the occasion. Fragrant Jade was disappointed to find that it was just another meeting. The graduating class sang, and a man talked a long time. She did not listen. After that, one of the graduates almost made her cry by making a sad little speech called "Farewell to Our Teachers and Schoolmates." Finally the graduates were called one by one to get their diplomas. They bowed to the principal and walked across the platform while the audience clapped. Now Fragrant Jade understood why Teacher Ho had wanted to get her foot straightened. She would have died of embarrassment to have had to limp across that platform!

In the afternoon, the graduates were given a farewell party by the younger girls. There was a program of funny dialogues and short plays that they had made up themselves. At the end, while they were eating fruit, cakes, and candy, and drinking tea, the chairman announced, "You may ask anyone for anything you like."

Someone called for Bright Wisdom to tell a story, and then they asked other girls for duets, or songs, or funny stories. Suddenly someone shouted, "Fragrant Jade, sing a song." Others joined, until it seemed as though the whole school was shouting "Fragrant Jade, sing a song." Her mind was empty. She could not think of any song at all, to say nothing of one that would be appropriate to sing at a party.

True Pearl came running to whisper, "Sing 'Lady Moon'." It was a favorite when the two of them sat on the grass by the moat, but it was such an easy little song! "Go on! Sing it quickly!" True Pearl urged.

As Fragrant Jade walked without limping to the platform, she was conscious of hundreds of eyes watching her. How glad she was that her foot was straight! When she stood before them, she could feel her knees trembling, but as soon as she began to sing, she was not frightened any more. There was nothing hard about singing "Lady Moon"!

That night the Third Court girls had the last evening prayers of the term. They sang a dozen hymns—there were no lessons to prepare—and then Miss Chang thanked the Heavenly Father for the good year they had had together. Fragrant Jade wanted to cry, to think it was over, but she was happy, too, and while Miss Chang was still praying, she said a little prayer all her own. It was just "Thank you, Heavenly Father, thank you, 'specially from me, because I have more than the other girls to be thankful for." You see, none of them had got a new straight foot.

The next morning, the Chen girls' father came in a heavy farm cart to take all four of the West Market girls home. They packed their bundles of clothes and comforters to make cushions against the sides of the cart, and put their washbasins holding their small toilet articles in a heap in the middle. Fragrant Jade packed her final examination papers carefully between her books. The teacher-mother had praised her because the grades were even better than at New Year's, in spite of the time she had spent in the hospital. It was really True Pearl who had accomplished that, Fragrant Jade thought gratefully, coming every day the way she had, and explaining everything so clearly. Fragrant Jade wrapped her books neatly in a square of blue cloth and put them into the cart.

On the way, the girls nibbled from a parcel of watermelon seeds and hard candy that they had saved from the farewell party. The springless cart seemed to hit every bump, and they had no protection from the sun, but they laughed and chattered and ignored the discomfort. Fragrant Jade did not tell her friends what she was thinking. She would watch her father's face when he first saw her foot, to see whether or not he was angry. If he could only know what a difference it made to her, not having to limp, she was sure he could not mind that it was a "foreign-devil doctor" who had made the foot straight. She was dreading meeting her sister-in-law, too. Being snubbed every day was not a pleasant prospect.

When West Market dogs began to announce their arrival, small boys and girls appeared, and then ran to spread the news. Fragrant Jade used to watch the road just that way when she was little. By the time the cart reached True Pearl's home, twenty or more children and grown-ups had gathered with her family to welcome the travelers. It was the hottest part of the day. The men were at home from the fields. All four girls climbed down from the cart to greet their friends, and to help unload True Pearl's bundles. Then they walked beside it along the village road, bowing to neighbors who had come out to their gateways to stand and watch the excitement.

"Look at Fragrant Jade's foot!" the children beside them called to each new group they approached. She walked tall and straight in her leather shoes. At every door she was commented on by amazed women. Who would have believed that her foot could be straightened when they all knew she had been born with it bent over!

Then, ahead, was her own home, with all the family—except Sister-in-law, she instantly noticed—waiting to welcome her. In her throat was a lump she could not swallow. When she was near enough, she stopped, stood with her feet together, and bowed to them, calling each by name, "Grandfather, Father, Mother, Big Brother, Second Brother." Then she looked at her father's face.

He was not angry! And her mother was smiling, pleased and proud.

Big Brother and Second Brother carried into the house the bundles she gave them. Several neighbor women came, and were talking to her mother. Fragrant Jade picked up her blue parcel of books.

"Our family thanks you for bringing our daughter," she heard her father say to Mr. Chen. "At a busy time, to take a day off from the fields and tire your mule with a trip to town is not a small thing."

"I had to go anyway for my own girls," Mr. Chen answered affably. "One more in the cart made no difference."

"I won't forget," Fragrant Jade heard her father answer. "It'll be my turn to take 'em back in the fall."

She stood tense, listening. Did that really mean—?

"It was never my idea to send her to school in the first place," her father grumbled. "I didn't think much of Christians, so I wasn't anxious to send her amongst 'em. I hope you won't laugh at me when I tell you I think she's turning out all the better for it. I've even been

getting acquainted with the preacher here. A lot of what he says
is real good sense, and he spends his time doing good."

"I've quizzed my girls, too, and the more I learn about the Christians the less I have to say against them."

"They care what happens to people, and try to make things better.
The preacher says that the Jesus they think so much of puts 'em up to
it. Take that idea of straightening our little cripple's foot. They
managed to do it so it didn't cost me a cent, and I took it as a real
kindness."

"Yes, and if she's going to be educated—"

"That's another thing! My girl's mother got it into her head that
the child has to learn to be a scholar. You know what a woman's
like when she gets a notion! If it had been one of the boys, I wouldn't
have been able to spare him from the fields, but a little girl doesn't
amount to anything. We don't need her around, so I suppose I'll
keep on wasting money on schooling for years to come."

"My girls say she's fine in her lessons."

"Well, of course that's part of it. It isn't just that her mother wants
her to go. I haven't any learning, but it appears to me that you
couldn't expect a child to become much of a scholar if she herself
didn't want to be. I didn't make any bargain with this one, but last
term her examination papers gave her mother and me considerable
face. If the ones she brings back this time are as good as those were,
I'll reckon that the child has done her part and I'll do mine."

Fragrant Jade hugged the examination papers she was carrying.
She had the answer to the problem she had been unable to solve. How
clear it was now! She had tried to think of something brave and
startling to do for her father. Like all Chinese fathers, for genera-
tions, who had waited to hear how their sons had done in the emperor's examinations, her father, too, hoped his child would stand
near the top. The thing she had brought her father, good grades, was
the thing he wanted most.

As Fragrant Jade walked through the gate into her home courtyard, she felt a happiness she could not have expressed. She was not
fooled by her father's remark about the uselessness of little girls. He
had praised her above anything she had ever dreamed. He had ac-
cepted her as the scholar in his family.

CHAPTER TEN

THE NEXT MORNING Fragrant Jade woke to the wonderful feeling of a long, long holiday stretching ahead, with school at the end of it.

It was June, but in the early morning, not too hot. She could hear the voices of her mother and Sister-in-law, up long since, and busy with the house work. The men had gone to the fields at daybreak, to put in many hours before the heat of the day, when they would come in for a rest. Sister-in-law might be irritating, but if Mrs. Chou had not had her as a new helper, Fragrant Jade would have been ashamed to lie in bed so late. As it was, she need not hurry. She stretched lazily.

How happy she was in her father's promise that she could go to school! In memory she went over all his words, as if they were a gift that she could see and feel. She had everything she wanted, she gloated to herself. Well, almost everything, she amended, hearing her sister-in-law's voice in the courtyard, and conscious that since her return yesterday her sister-in-law had utterly ignored her.

"I'll just ignore her, too," she promised herself, and then recalled the advice Bright Wisdom had given her, and her own intention to endure patiently almost anything in order to keep her mother happy. After all, she would be going away again at the end of the summer.

After a while she got up and went out into the familiar courtyard. The apricot tree was full of fruit, and though it was not yet very ripe, she found six or seven pretty ones that were not too green.

Suddenly someone on the road yelled for a donkey to stop, and then pounded on the big front gate. Fragrant Jade ran to open it, and found a strange young man who looked like a farmer.

"Is the daughter-in-law in this house a Li from Pinetree Village?"

Sister-in-law came running. She knew him, but before she could make any polite speeches, he panted, "I had some business north of here, and since I was coming through West Market, I brought you word from home!"

The news must be very bad to make this young man talk about it so abruptly without making first a few general remarks about this or that. Fragrant Jade could see that Sister-in-law was frightened. "What's—what's happened?" she stuttered.

"Your mother didn't send me, because you can't do anything about it, but since I was coming by . . . "

"Quickly! What's happened?"

"This morning your brother started out early to take a load of wheat to market, and he hadn't gone far when a dog scared that mean mule of his, and it started to run away. Your brother tried to get to its head to stop it, and fell under the wheels."

"*Ai-ya!*" Sister-in-law began to wail. She could guess the rest "What will my mother do?" she cried, "With my father dead, we've only my brother to work in the fields . . . and so many children's mouths to feed!"

Mrs. Chou had come to hear what was going on, and now that her daughter-in-law was crying so hard, she undertook to find out from the young man more about the accident.

"It's terrible!" he said. "The cart ran over both legs and broke them both, one above and one below the knee, and the bones stick out through the skin. He's lost an awful lot of blood. The older folks say they never knew of anyone's living more than a few days after such a bad break, and if he does, it's a sure thing he'll never work in a field again."

Hearing this, Sister-in-law cried even louder than before, so that his voice was lost in the uproar she made.

"Broken bones?" Fragrant Jade thought. Dr. Lo had said, "I like to fix up people's broken bones for them."

"Mother! Dr. Lo can fix his legs. He likes to!"

Mrs. Chou considered the idea, and then shook her head. "Dr. Lo would never come all this way."

"They can take Sister-in-law's brother to the hospital. I saw men carrying a sick person on a door, and Nurse Chi said that country people bring patients that way all the time."

Fragrant Jade felt so certain of what to do, and was in such a hurry to do it, that she was impatient with Sister-in-law who could hardly be persuaded to stop crying so they could discuss plans. Mrs. Chou's faith grew as they talked, and finally Sister-in-law, too, was convinced.

Less than half an hour later, the two girls were hurrying along the footpaths between the fields, already in sight of Pinetree Village. Sister-in-law was so anxious that, in spite of her tiny bound feet, she

made Fragrant Jade, in her stiff leather shoes, hurry to keep up. Their
faces were red with the heat. Neither of them said anything. They
were not thinking about themselves, but about the young man they
hoped to help.

Most of the inhabitants of the village had crowded into the Li
courtyard, and were discussing the accident in loud tones. Sister-in-
law pushed her way through and Fragrant Jade squeezed after, into
a tiny room, also full of people. On the brick bed was a terrible sight.
Covered with blood, the injured young man lay unconscious, groaning
dismally. The rest of the brick bed was full of his mother and
younger sisters, rocking back and forth and wailing hoarsely. Sister-
in-law showed no signs of what she must have felt. At home, on first
hearing the news, she had acted utterly helpless. Now she was quite
changed.

"Mother, I have come," she announced in a tone respectful but
firm.

"Ai-ya! Ai-ya!" her mother wailed more loudly, recognizing the
familiar voice. Then uncovering her eyes, she began to tell, in broken
sentences, of their appalling misfortune.

"I know all about it," Sister-in-law interrupted. "We're going to
send Brother to the hospital as fast as we can."

The other people in the room stopped talking to listen.

"There's a foreign-devil doctor," she went on, "that can fix his
legs. If you don't believe it, look at my little sister's foot that used
to be bent over, and now is as straight as anybody's."

The people in the courtyard were trying to crowd into the room.

"Come, Fragrant Jade, come outside the door and stand on a bench
where everyone can see your foot."

Fragrant Jade climbed up and stood on an old table where they
could all see her. "Isn't it so!" an old woman's voice commented
shrilly. "That's the Chou's Little Crooked-foot. I've seen her before.
She was born with one foot bent over on the side, but look at it
now!"

"The American doctor can fix my brother's legs, too." Sister-in-law
spoke clearly in the silence that followed. "We must send him quickly,
before he gets worse. Won't any of you neighbors help to carry
him?"

Instantly they offered, and began to plan how to do it.

"We'll need a letter to the doctor. Somebody run quick and ask
Elder Teacher Wang to write one," one neighbor suggested.

"Oh, no," Sister-in-law stopped them. "Fragrant Jade can write, and she knows the doctor, too. Hurry, Little Sister, while we get my brother ready."

Mrs. Li, in the inner room was objecting. "They mustn't take him away from home to die," she wailed. "He must die here where his father did."

The neighbors all helped, now there was something they could do. Some talked to Mrs. Li, persuading her to let her son go. Others ran to get ropes and carrying poles. They called in from the fields the strongest young men in the village, double the number needed, so that by taking turns they could make the long tiring trip to the hospital as fast as possible.

At school Fragrant Jade had not yet studied the proper forms for letter writing, but she had some idea how a letter ought to sound, and could write the characters that were necessary. She found a bit of paper and a pencil, and wrote:

DR. LO, GREAT ONE:
Please do not be angry with my Sister-in-law's brother that he has broken both his legs. His trouble means that you must weary yourself and waste your heart. I have guaranteed your skill to my sister-in-law's family, so to keep me from losing face, please take him into your hospital and cure him. They have not very much money, but when they have sold their wheat they will pay you as much as they can.

							I bow to you,
									FRAGRANT JADE.

She could not write very fast. By the time she had finished, the men were ready to start. They had laid the injured man on a wooden door which hung by ropes across the shoulders of the carriers, two at the head and two at the feet. A blue cotton cloth hanging from the poles kept the sun off his face.

"We'll hurry as fast as we can, and tonight we'll bring you word again," they promised Mrs. Li. "Don't make yourself sick being anxious. It'll be all right."

"Yes, yes, it'll be all right," the neighbors assured her, as confidently as if his going had been their own idea.

Fragrant Jade and Sister-in-law did not linger. Again, without saying much to each other, they trudged back through the fields to report to Mrs. Chou all they had done.

Four days later, Sister-in-law was sitting sadly in the courtyard, mending something. No word had come about her brother. The family had tried to cheer her by telling her that he must still be living, or surely she would have heard.

Fragrant Jade started to climb the tree to gather some apricots.

"I'll help you," Sister-in-law offered. It was not the first time during these four days that she had done something for Fragrant Jade. A shy friendliness was on her face.

They found plenty of ripe ones. When Fragrant Jade climbed down, she divided the apricots into two equal piles. "Half of them are yours," she said.

Sister-in-law left them lying beside her, and went on sewing. She did not eat any, but she looked pleased.

After a little Mr. Chou and his sons came in from the fields for their noonday rest. They had nothing to say, but when the younger men went into the house, Mr. Chou was still tinkering with a farm implement near the front gate. So when, as on the other day, there was the sound of someone arriving on donkey-back he opened the gate. It was the same young farmer who had come before from Pine-tree Village. When Sister-in-law saw him, she ran toward him.

"No, I haven't time," he said when he was asked in, "but I've been to the hospital and seen her brother." As was proper, he spoke only to Mr. Chou, and merely jerked his head in the direction of the young woman who was most closely interested in his news.

"How is he?" Mr. Chou and his daughter-in-law both asked at once.

"For the likes of me, it's a miracle."

"You mean he's better?" "Did you see him?" Again they both spoke at once.

"Yes, he's getting along fine—no fever, and he can eat. He's inside some sort of framework that he says doesn't feel good, but he says he can stand it."

"But—but will he always be a cripple?" Sister-in-law asked breathlessly.

"No, the doctor says it'll take several months, but there's no reason why he won't get entirely well so he'll be like other people. To me it would look as though that doctor is a very clever man."

"Isn't it so!" Sister-in-law exclaimed, delighted.

Mr. Chou put his hand on Fragrant Jade's shoulder. "This is already the second time this neighborhood of ours has got advantage from knowing that doctor. It was no mistake for this little girl to bring the news of him."

The young man and Sister-in-law with their quick "Yes, Yes," ac-

cepted the word as praise, and so did Fragrant Jade, her cheeks flushing with pleasure. Their caller turned to get on his donkey. "Don't worry about your mother and your little sisters. The neighbors'll help with the crops."

When he had left, and Mr. Chou without further remarks, had gone into the house, Fragrant Jade brought her apricots and sat down near where Sister-in-law was again taking up her sewing. She could not remember ever before having been so happy.

"Such good news!" Sister-in-law exclaimed.

"I hoped we'd hear something good pretty soon," Fragrant Jade told her sympathetically. She was proud that her Dr. Lo had been able to fix the broken bones.

"And I keep thinking that if it hadn't been for you, my brother would surely have died. Then what would my mother and little sisters have done?"

"Oh, but it wasn't my doing! I couldn't have helped a bit if you hadn't gone over there and managed them all so well. All I did was to tell you about the doctor."

"That's what I'm talking about! Your father kept claiming that he didn't want you to go to boarding school. But now he's glad, and I'm glad that we have a girl student in our family. Your heart is kind, and you're not stuck on yourself." She smiled as she spoke, and her eyes were full of good will, like Bright Wisdom's.

Fragrant Jade smiled back. She believed that she and Sister-in-law were going to be friends after all.

She smelled the prettiest of the apricots she had spread in her lap, and took a big bite. "How comfortable it is," she thought, "where everybody likes everybody else."